DEATH TRAP

DEATH TRAP

A MURDER MYSTERY

Charles J Thayer

Chartwell Publications
Palm City, Florida

www.ChartwellPublications.com

ISBN: 9781729171332

DEATH TRAP

A MURDER MYSTERY

This story is a work of fiction

DEDICATION

Molly & Linda

For Your Encouragement and Patience

Thank You

PROLOG

My name is Steve Wilson. I recently retired as senior auditor at one of our nation's largest banks. My retirement planning consisted of traveling to Maine to unwind, enjoy the scenery and write a murder mystery novel. In other words, I really had no plan.

"Life is like a box of chocolates,
you never know what you're gonna get"

Forrest Gump

Little did I know my curiosity about a deserted lobster boat, a dead lobsterman and three missing photos would put my own life in danger.

1

1st Week of August

Thursday afternoon and I was enjoying a beer on the upstairs deck of the Fisherman's restaurant in Stone Harbor, Maine. The restaurant's waterfront deck overlooks the lobster boats moored out in the harbor and the town dock where the boats unload their daily catch.

I had driven to Maine following my retirement in mid-June after thirty-five years as senior auditor for one of our nation's largest banks. Fisherman's is just a short walk down the town's main street from the Stone Harbor Inn, my home for the next six weeks.

I had enjoyed an afternoon beer in the Fisherman's downstairs Pub my first day in Stone Harbor and discovered it was a gathering spot for some of the local lobstermen after they returned to the harbor to unload their catch. I was clearly an outsider in the Pub that first afternoon and I was now more comfortable having my afternoon beer on the deck above the Pub.

The lobstermen were still "fresh" off their lobster boats and easy to identify by their work clothes and rubber boots. In nice weather most of them moved outside to picnic tables located below the upstairs deck after they ordered something to eat and drink.

I had also discovered that sitting on the upstairs deck gave me a unique opportunity to eavesdrop as a series of unusual events unfolded during my stay in Stone Harbor.

The local lobstermen's conversations had become very somber that Thursday afternoon as one of the local lobster boats owned by a man named Rob was found drifting with no one aboard. The boat, named the Mary Alice, had been spotted by Captain Max and his mate Clyde. Max now was the center of attention.

"We saw Rob's boat and noticed he wasn't working his traps, boat just seemed to be sitting dead in the water with the engine running but not moving."

"I pulled along side and called out to see if he was OK. Thought he must be in his cabin as I didn't see anyone on deck."

"No answer, so I decided to climb onboard and I discovered Rob was not on his boat. Damn boat was deserted!"

I didn't know it then but my curiosity about that deserted lobster boat would start me on an unpredictable and very dangerous odyssey.

# # #

This was my first visit to Maine. I had selected Maine as the place for me to unwind based on recommendations from friends that had vacationed in Maine for many years. In early July I had rented a car and departed my home in New York City with plans to enjoy Portland's restaurant scene for a week. I then headed 'DownEast' to enjoy the remainder of July in B&Bs while participating in typical tourist activities in Boothbay, Camden and Bar Harbor.

DownEast Maine Waterfront

DownEast Maine is that section of Maine's coast that extends mostly eastward from Camden to the Canadian boarder. I took side trips to tour the smaller coastal towns of Tenants Harbor, Belfast, Castine, Blue Hill, Stonington and Northeast Harbor as I drove between my B&Bs along US1, Maine's coastal highway.

My friends were right. A small coastal town in Maine appeared to make an excellent location to unwind and contemplate my future retirement. No question, I needed to stop and think about how I would now occupy my time.

Over time my audit specialty had focused on financial crimes and my career at the bank progressed rapidly. It seems I had a talent for both respecting customer privacy requirements and yet deciphering suspicious transactions. My analytical skills had helped identify and shut down some very sophisticated programs for fraud, insider trading, Ponzi schemes and money laundering.

During my professional career I had written hundreds of detailed reports describing criminal activity and I planned to write a murder mystery based on some of my past experiences. I enjoy reading mystery novels and have attended a number of author lectures in New York over the years. At a recent event, I asked the author:

"If I want to write a murder mystery how would you suggest I start?"

He replied; "First, it's very hard to write fiction. Distraction will be your worst enemy. Get away to a small town with nothing to do and just write it."

I had decided to take this author's advice and selected the Stone Harbor Inn based on a recommendation from a couple who had stayed at the Inn several times in the past. They had assured me that the rooms were comfortable, the food was excellent and the views were terrific.

This was first my week in Stone Harbor. I had booked a room at the Inn for six weeks and had arrived Sunday evening. When I arrived I was greeted with a friendly;

"Good evening Mr. Wilson, I am Mrs. Baxter, owner of the Inn. Please call me Anne."

Anne was a tall, attractive brunette that appeared to be several years younger than me and although she offered a very friendly greeting she was also businesslike in her appearance and actions.

After I had filled out and signed my registration card, Anne directed me to my room which had a small desk, nice double bed, private bath and a great view of the harbor. In response to her questions at registration, I had indicated I was a recently retired senior bank auditor on vacation.

Over time I had developed the habit of only sharing limited information about the nature of my profession. Thankfully, most people had little interest in discussing something that sounded as boring as auditing and accounting.

Monday morning Anne had greeted me with another warm welcome;

"Good morning Mr. Wilson, I hope your room was satisfactory."

"It's very nice, thank you."

"We have a selection of breakfast items including fruit, pastry, juice and coffee available every morning. We also provide at least one hot selection each morning and this morning it's blueberry pancakes with eggs of your choice."

"Thank you, the pancakes and some scrambled eggs sound wonderful."

Other guests were also having breakfast on this beautiful, early August morning. An older couple was discussing their grandchildren, a younger couple was preoccupied with viewing their cell phones and an attractive blonde woman at least ten years younger than myself was sitting alone.

On the way to my table Anne introduced me to the other guests.

"Mr. and Mrs. Johnson, please meet Steve Wilson our newest guest. Steve is a retired accountant from New York City." The Johnsons were delightful people visiting from Virginia and we enjoyed a brief visit about their grandchildren.

"Mr. and Mrs. Smith, please meet Steve Wilson our newest guest." Our greeting was briefly acknowledged before they returned to their cell phone activities. I learned they were both attorneys from Boston and both certainly seemed preoccupied with their work. They didn't look very relaxed for a vacation.

"Mr. Wilson please meet Nancy Olson." During our brief introduction I learned that Nancy was a college professor from Missouri who had checked in over the weekend and would be attending a three-week photography workshop at the Shoreside Art Camp located a few miles out of town.

Anne served the blueberry pancakes to both the Johnsons and me but I assumed she had some help in the kitchen. Anne had also told me when I arrived on Sunday that I might occasionally encounter Sally, a local teenager she had hired to help her at the Inn, change the guests' bedding and clean their bathrooms.

The Inn was a converted, historical sea captain's home located on the town's main street across from the waterfront with four private guest rooms, the breakfast room and a small living room with comfortable seating, a fireplace and a small desk with some information about Stone Harbor.

Anne had a small office just inside the front door with a desk for registration but no computer. The

Inn did not serve alcohol but guests could bring wine and other beverages to the living room during their stay if they so desired.

#   #   #

After breakfast I took a long walk for exercise. My morning routine in New York City included a stop at a gym before I walked to my office at the bank. I stand just a little over six feet tall and this routine helped keep me trim with my weight just below 200 pounds. My temporary routine in Stone Harbor would soon be long walks and the friendly folks around town began waving at this stranger with dark hair and a blue baseball cap each morning.

That first morning I explored the small community of Stone Harbor along the waterfront main street and visited the occasional art gallery, souvenir shop, general store and the local library. Reading has always been an important pastime for me and I was impressed that a small community like Stone Harbor had such a nice library with a wide selection of books and a section in the front window to exhibit community projects and activities.

Stone Harbor's economy was based on lobster fishing and its reputation as a working lobster town attracted daily tourist visits but the Inn was one of the few places a visitor could stay overnight. My primary mission on that first morning walk was to identify convenient restaurants for lunch and dinner as the Inn only served breakfast.

There were only a couple of local cafes that served lunch and as I wanted to stay along the waterfront I selected the Waterfront Cafe for lunch that first day. When I sat at the counter that first time I was greeted with;

" Hi, I'm Sandy, what's your name?"

"My name's Steve."

"I can tell you are 'from away' - where's your home?"

"I live in New York City."

"Just visiting for the day?"

"No, I am staying down at the Inn for the next six weeks. It's a really nice location."

"That's a long vacation. What do you do?"

"I'm retired, I was an auditor at a bank."

I thought it only fair to ask a few questions in return.

"How long have you lived in Stone Harbor?"

"Born and raised here like most folks in town."

"Do you get many tourists?"

"Mostly day trippers just to look at the lobster boats. They want to tell folks back home they visited a real lobster town and they order one of our lobster rolls for lunch."

Sandy was a trim blonde that appeared to be in her mid-twenties and was wearing a blue polo shirt with the cafe logo with her blue jeans. People at the cafe were inquisitive but more open and friendly than my neighbors in New York City and when I asked Sandy a general question almost everyone at the counter would join in with additional information.

The town folks shared local news with Sandy giving me an opportunity to eavesdrop on those conversations and learn a little more about activities in the community. It didn't take long to learn that Sandy was a local gossip and more than willing to exchange information with the other folks at the counter with a "Don't say I told you but ———". It was clear that her friends at the counter were also more than willing to share information with Sandy with the same "Don't say I told you".

I was somewhat amazed that Sandy and her friends didn't seem to concern themselves with my presence and would occasionally even include me in a conversation.

It seems every seaside town in Maine has a "Fisherman's" restaurant and Stone Harbor was no exception. I found Fisherman's just a short walk down the town's waterfront street from the Inn. The upstairs restaurant had an inside dining room with doors to an outside covered deck with more tables that overlooked the harbor.

That deck was where I overheard Captain Max describe finding the deserted lobster boat. The deck also had separate outside steps that I could use when the restaurant was closed in the mornings and I had decided it would make an excellent outdoor hangout for quiet mornings with my notebook and laptop to work on my novel before the restaurant opened for lunch.

DownEast Maine Harbor

The deck was also a perfect spot overlooking the harbor for an afternoon beer and I was thankful it had a extensive menu for dinner as it was the only restaurant along the waterfront serving dinner in the evening. I must confess I frequently ordered an entree that contained lobster from their menu.

On my second visit to the deck I was again greeted by the waitress:

"Hi, remember my name is Kathy, nice to see you again. You want the same beer you had yesterday?"

"Yes, thank you, that will be fine."

Kathy retuned with my beer and asked; "What's your name?"

"I'm Steve."

"Most folks only visit for the day, you staying in town?"

"Yes, down at the Inn."

"You on vacation? How long you plan to stay?"

"Actually I am retired and I plan to stay a couple of weeks."

"Well enjoy the view and your beer. I got to take care of those folks that just sat down."

Like Sandy at the cafe, Kathy was also trim and appeared to be in her mid-twenties but she had dark hair in a pony tail and was wearing a green polo shirt with the Fisherman's logo with her blue jeans. After she had served the other table I asked her about their shirts and Kathy replied;

"Thanks for asking. We sell our coffee mugs and these shirts in different colors to the visitors so we wear them as advertising. Want to buy one?"

"Sure, I'll pick out a shirt to buy today."

Starting that first week, Kathy would bring my afternoon beer without asking when I sat at a table. I could overhear the lobstermen's conversations when they went outside below the deck after they ordered something to eat and drink. I sometimes felt a little guilty being an eavesdropper but I was generally intrigued by their conversation and the challenges they faced.

The lobstermen's conversations covered about everything you can imagine - the price of lobster, sports, politics, weather, boats, women and the upcoming lobster boat races. At first I couldn't imagine what happened at a lobster boat race but this would change in a couple of weeks when the races occurred over a weekend in Stone Harbor.

I certainly knew nothing about owning and running a lobster boat but it's clearly a tough occupation and bad weather or fog was no excuse for staying in port. During my stay in Stone Harbor I became increasingly impressed with the independent nature, courage and dedication of these lobstermen.

I didn't know it that first week but eavesdropping at the Waterfront Cafe and on the Fisherman's deck over the Pub would put my own life in serious danger.

2

Max had discovered the deserted lobster boat Thursday morning during my first week in Stone Harbor and he had shared the details of that morning with his friends in the Pub that afternoon.

Max explained; "No answer, so I decided to climb onboard and found Rob was not on his boat. Damn boat was deserted!"

"So you guys heard me call the Coast Guard on my radio and they told us to search around Rob's boat to see if he might have gone overboard."

"Damn fools, told them that's what we were already doing but we hadn't seen anything or anyone in the water. Told them several nearby boats had also joined our search but there was no sign of Rob in the water."

"The Coast Guard told us to stay with Rob's boat until they arrived. Damn, we had to wait another hour when we could have been working and emptying some of my traps."

"While I was waiting I took a couple of pictures on his boat with my phone but I didn't really see nothing suspicious."

Max told the group that when the Coast Guard arrived they also took photos of Rob's boat and then took photos, fingerprints and statements from both Clyde and himself. He was also required to provide copies of the photos he had taken to the Coast Guard.

"Damn Coast Guard treated us like we were criminals!"

The Coast Guard had then towed Rob's boat into the town dock where I could see the lobster boat was currently located.

The Coast Guard had told Max they had alerted the local sheriff's office and the local deputy sheriff had met the boat at the town dock when it arrived. The deputy had placed the standard yellow tape on the boat indicating "do not enter" and he had told Max that Rob's boat was to remain in his official custody for several more days.

Apparently the local deputy had called Rob's wife, Mary Alice, during the time Rob's boat was being towed to the town dock.

"That young deputy told me Mary Alice said Rob had left the house early that morning to go to his boat as usual before she got up. She didn't know why the boat was adrift and had not heard from Rob."

"Deputy said Mary Alice was worried and tried to call Rob on her cell phone but he didn't answer so she left a message. Deputy told her to call him when she heard from Rob."

The men at the Pub were speculating about every possible reason for the deserted boat - it was the topic of the day.

"Mighty strange, do you think that boy just fell overboard? That water's damn cold."

Max replied; "Hard to tell but we looked all around that area and didn't see him in the water."

"That boy's been acting kinda strange recently. Stupid to fire Danny and start working alone."

"What about drugs? You know the DEA boarded and searched his boat a couple of times. Didn't find nothin."

"Never could understand why he stopped unloading at the town dock and started selling to those independent guys."

"He must've been doing OK, since I heard he paid cash for that new silver pickup."

In most respects, it sounded to me like Rob had become somewhat of a loner and had disassociated himself from the local group.

I could identify Max's unique voice from that first conversation and it appeared he was seen as kind of an older, informal leader of this local group of lobstermen.

Someone asked; "Max, did you notice that life jacket hanging on that hook? You think Rob might not have being wearing one?"

Max responded; "That's a possibility. But that water's so cold that Rob wouldn't survive for more than an hour even this time of year. Only good a life jacket does is help searchers find the body."

I could tell from their voices the lobstermen were worried about Rob and hoped he would somehow turn up with an explanation.

Max added; "No point in letting any lobsters just sit in Rob's traps. We ought to just pick a few up and give the lobsters to Mary Alice."

Although apparently very rare, someone in the group speculated that Rob might have gotten careless with his mooring and his boat could simply have slipped its mooring line in his absence.

Max responded; "Doubt it, the engine was running on the boat and the deputy told me Rob's truck was parked at his dock and his dinghy was tied to the mooring. Somebody was on that boat."

#   #   #

On Saturday afternoon the group was in shock and Max was again the center of attention. Max and Clyde were out as usual that morning hauling their lobster traps when they also spotted some of Rob's lobster buoys. So they started hauling a few of Rob's lobster traps to give the catch to Mary Alice. Max told the group they had encountered an extra heavy trap that nearly damaged their gear.

"I thought that trap was caught on something like an abandoned anchor or something and I was just about ready to tell Clyde to give up when I spotted something below the surface. We continued to haul the trap and were shocked when Rob's body surfaced."

"Clyde and I dragged Rob's body aboard and discovered the damn fool's boot had been caught in a wrap of his lobster trap's buoy line. Looks like he got pulled overboard by the lobster trap he had tossed from his boat. He wasn't wearing his life vest and drowned in those heavy work clothes."

"We noted the location with our GPS and I called the sheriff's office on my cell phone - didn't want to broadcast what we found on the radio."

"The deputy sheriff contacted the Coast Guard and we wasted another hour waiting for them to arrive. Man them folks was official - really treated us like criminals this time! They took a bunch of photos, took our statements and even took our fingerprints again! Gave me a real bad time about pulling Rob's trap just because I hadn't requested official permission!"

"They didn't want to move Rob's body until we got back to the town dock and met the deputy. Damn spooky having that Coast Guard officer and Rob's body on my boat. Damn glad when they took it down to the funeral home."

"And, to make matters worse they want to inspect my boat and won't let me have it back until Tuesday!"

"Deputy told me they will need to send Rob's body to the State Medical Examiner to determine the cause of death. Seems like a waste of time to me, boy drowned."

I could hear that Max was again sharing his photos with the group and the initial consensus was a tragic accident had occurred as a result of Rob's decision to start working alone. Their conversations indicated the photos showed the line had wrapped around Rob's boot just a couple of feet from the lobster trap. Someone then started talking about a gash that was visible on the side of Rob's head.

"Notice that gash on Rob's head? From that gash it looks like he must have hit his head on the side of his boat when he was pulled overboard by the lobster trap. Guess that's why he was unable to recover and drowned."

"Funny he would hit his head. Remember what happened a couple years ago? Charley got caught by a line and broke his damn leg when it hit the side of the boat but he managed to save himself. How the hell did Rob hit his head?"

"You gotta point. Don't see anything wrong with Rob's legs, just that line wrapped around his boot. That line around his boot should have pulled his leg into the side of the boat, not his head."

Max then told the group he and Clyde had been pulling traps close to an area that was also claimed by lobstermen running boats from a nearby island.

"I noticed some of Rob's lobster buoys next to mine and decided to pull a few while I was out there. You know the island boats claim that's their territory, not ours, and they don't like us putting our traps out there. I never been harassed but I heard rumors that some of the island's boats had started harassing Rob after he started working alone and possibly cut the lines to some of Rob's traps."

"You think Rob could have had trouble the other day? That head gash looks mighty suspicious."

"You know, Rob had a bit of a temper and could have got gotten into a serious argument or fight with one of those island boats. If something bad happened those boys could've decided to cover up Rob's death by faking an accident."

Max calmed the situation; "Let's don't start more trouble than we want. Let's see what that Medical Examiner has to say. No need to start a new lobster war if Rob's death was an accident."

Frankly, I was impressed that Max didn't let the beer and their emotions take control of the situation with potentially false accusations. Max sounded tough but fair.

#   #   #

I was intrigued by this discussion of a potential lobster war in a disputed area. Was this lobster fishing business really so competitive that the lobstermen would resort to violence? From my perspective, sitting on the Fisherman's deck that first week, it certainly appeared to be a tough business but I had the impression from their conversations it was more like a large, local family.

Nearly all of these lobstermen seemed to be born and raised in or near Stone Harbor and many referred to their relatives in their conversations. I frequently overheard references to "father", "brother", "uncle", or "cousin" when they referred to other local lobstermen.

To my initial surprise I also overheard references to my "sister" or "aunt" and it was evident that some of the local women also worked on the lobster boats. These lobstermen also seemed to like and respect a Captain Peggy who would occasionally join them for a beer at the Pub.

DownEast Town Dock

I had a great view of the town dock from the Fisherman's deck and could watch the local lobster boats offload their daily catch in the afternoon. The lobster boats would come to the town dock to unload their lobsters and large refrigerated trucks would take the live lobsters away, I assumed to a distribution center.

The lobstermen would then return their boats to a mooring in the harbor and return by dinghy to the smaller floating dingy dock reserved for them next to the town dock.

I had already observed that Maine has tides that reach ten feet so floating docks were certainly necessary for docking their dinghies. The commercial docks for unloading lobster tended to be much larger and small cranes were used to lift crates with live lobsters up from the lobster boats to the dock.

Lobster Boats on Moorings

I would frequently overhear heated discussions between the lobstermen about sports or other topics. The Boston teams were a frequent topic of rather loud discussion but at the end of the day everyone shared a beer. I was shocked when the conversation speculated about the potential for violence with lobstermen from another town.

#   #   #

After dinner I returned to my room at the Inn and undertook some online research on "lobster wars" and conflicts over fishing areas.

I discovered several old news reports about lobster wars and that some of those conflicts had even included gunfire. It certainly appeared that lobstermen could fight to protect fishing areas they considered to belong to them.

My research indicated that lobstermen are licensed to fish in one of seven zones; however, they may set traps anywhere in the approved zone. Maine has no areas that are actually assigned within a zone to specific lobster boats. All such agreements are informal understandings between neighboring towns and islands. The borders are not marked and disputes could frequently occur.

My initial research helped open my eyes to the competitive nature of the lobster business and it certainly seemed possible that Rob had been a victim of conflict over lobster fishing territory.

3

2nd Week of August

On Monday afternoon of the following week, Mary Alice, Rob's distraught widow, appeared at the Pub. I was sitting out on the Fisherman's deck and clearly heard her bizarre accusations.

"I don't know why they did it? Just don't know!"

"Rob didn't do anything bad to them. Why? Why?"

"Rob can't get me new stuff now! I need more! Who can help me?"

This was clearly not a conversation any of the lobstermen wanted to have with Mary Alice. Captain Peggy was having a beer with the group that afternoon and she and one of the other lobstermen volunteered to take Mary Alice home. When they returned a short while later, Peggy expressed serious concern about Mary Alice's visit to the Pub and her apparent search for a new drug source now that Rob was dead.

"Mary Alice always seemed like a really nice girl, hard to believe she was looking for drugs."

The group's conversations again speculated that Rob and his wife had both gotten into a drug habit and the possibility that carelessness might have led to Rob's accidental death.

"If that boy was on drugs he could have screwed up and got himself tangled up in that buoy line."

"If he was on drugs why didn't they ever find any when they searched his boat?"

"More important, why was the DEA searching Rob's boat? They must have had some reason to do it more than once."

"Who the hell is 'they'? Mary Alice say anything more when you took her back home?"

Peggy responded; "Nope, all she would say was Rob told her he was having some trouble so she thought 'they' were responsible."

Peggy added; "Not sure what that girl was on but saw a couple of empty liquor bottles on her kitchen table. Looked like she had been doing some serious drinking."

"Who the hell is 'they'? She saying someone killed Rob?"

"Might be he told her about his problems with the island boats."

"Think they will find any drugs in Rob's body?"

"Like I said, if that boy was on drugs he might have got careless and got his damn foot caught in that buoy line."

Max concluded; "Hell, gonna be interesting to see what the Medical Examiner has to say."

#   #   #

At lunch on Tuesday the conversation was all about the visit to the Pub by Mary Alice. Sandy as usual was a wealth of gossip;

"Don't say I told you but Kathy told me Mary Alice showed up drunk at the Pub yesterday looking for drugs."

"Captain Peggy took her back home. Nobody wants to get involved with that kinda talk."

I was surprised that the lobstermen's conversations that afternoon avoided the topic of Mary Alice's visit the day before. Looked like Sandy was right, nobody really wanted to get involved in a public conversation about Mary Alice finding a new source for drugs.

#   #   #

On Wednesday morning at breakfast at the Inn, Anne embarrassed Nancy by announcing to the other guests;

"I received a call from Barbara out at the art camp last night that some of Nancy's photographs have been selected for display down at the library."

"The local art camp selects work from their best student from each class to share with our community and Nancy's work was selected as best in class!"

During my first week I had learned at breakfast that Nancy enjoyed taking photos very early in the morning before returning to the the Inn for her breakfast. She then would go the the Fisherman's deck to edit the photos on her Apple laptop before driving to her photography workshop at the art camp.

Nancy was obviously extremely talented but also very reserved and seemed preoccupied with her work. As a result, our morning conversations at breakfast or on the deck were always friendly but very brief.

I took this opportunity to suggest that Nancy and I walk together to the library to see the photo exhibit displayed in the library window before she headed out to her photography workshop.

The photos on display were several dozen, candid color photos that captured the splendor of coastal scenery, majesty of birds in flight, animals foraging in the woods and various working lobster boats in action. Nancy's photos were very artistic and had really balanced composition.

Nancy's excellent photos certainly highlighted Stone Harbor's unique character and I could understand why her photos had been selected. I assumed that Nancy must have an amazing telescopic lens and other photo equipment in her bag as many of her photos had to be taken just at dawn from some distance.

When I asked her about other photos, she proudly pulled out her iPad and scrolled through dozens of photos of boats, birds and landscapes she had taken for the workshop. Nancy then departed to thank her workshop's instructors.

#　　#　　#

Sandy was a wealth of information and gossip at lunch on Thursday.

"Have you heard? Neighbor found Mary Alice dead this morning with a needle next to her body. Looks like a drug overdose."

Everyone at the lunch counter appeared to have a theory but no facts. Like her husband, her body had been taken to the local funeral home and, due to the circumstances, was also being sent to the State Medical Examiner for an autopsy to confirm her cause of death.

That afternoon the lobstermen's conversation was all about Mary Alice and her suspected overdose. They were all very upset as Mary Alice was a local girl and many had known both Mary Alice and Rob since they were children.

This was really the first time I understood that Rob was part of the town's younger generation as many of the lobstermen in this group were older. I could hear that Captain Peggy was extremely upset.

"I should have done more. Known that girl since she was a child. How did she get those drugs after we took her home?"

"Her family is just crushed and I hear her brother Dave blames Rob for getting her into heroin."

Nobody had any answers and again nobody really wanted to explore the topic of drugs in much detail.

I no longer felt guilty about eavesdropping on Sandy's gossip at lunch or the lobstermen's conversations while sitting on the deck above the

Pub. After all, these are public places and I was seldom alone during my afternoons on the deck.

I knew from my work at the bank that illegal drug usage was a significant problem in parts of New England and the speculation about drugs also being involved in Rob's death was a possibility.

#   #   #

On my Friday afternoon walk, I stopped by the library again to admire Nancy's photo exhibit and discovered three of her photos were now missing from the display in the window. Stone Harbor's small library was only open for a few hours each day so I was unable to ask the librarian why they had been removed.

#   #   #

I was pleased to see Nancy at breakfast on Saturday morning and again complimented her on her talent. She was modest but obviously pleased with the recognition she had received when her workshop had selected her photographs for public display at the local library. She was puzzled when I asked;

"Why were three of your photos removed from your exhibit in the library window?"

"I have no idea, when did that happen?"

"I don't know. Just noticed on my afternoon walk yesterday but the library was closed. I can ask the librarian later this morning."

After breakfast we both adjourned to the Fisherman's deck as usual and she again focused on editing photos on her Apple laptop. That morning her work was interrupted by a call on her cell phone. Her expression turned dramatically from a smile to confusion and then panic. She abruptly grabbed her laptop and photo bag and headed across the street to her car and she quickly drove away.

I was surprised and somewhat concerned by her actions and assumed she had received some very unsettling news. As I departed I noticed that in her hurry Nancy had forgotten her iPad. I decided to pick it up so I could return it to her later that day.

On my walk to lunch, I stopped by the library to inquire about the missing photos and discovered the librarian was also puzzled and had no idea why the photos were now missing.

4

3rd Week of August

I was surprised when Nancy did not appear at breakfast Sunday morning. Anne also appeared surprised that Nancy was not there and had apparently not returned to the Inn the prior evening.

I told Anne about the phone call.

"Anne, when Nancy and I were over at the Fisherman's deck yesterday morning she got a phone call that seemed to upset her. After she hung up she just got up, walked to her car and drove away."

Worried, Anne then called Barbara out at the art camp.

Barbara confirmed; "Anne, Nancy is not here and she didn't show up for her workshop yesterday. I assumed she had just stayed in town for some reason."

Anne replied; "No, Nancy apparently received a phone call with some bad news and just drove off yesterday morning. Let me know when you hear from her and I will do the same."

Nancy had already paid Anne for her room since the workshop still had a week to go. We all speculated that Nancy would either return in a few days or contact Barbara at the art camp or Anne about her belongings.

I took that opportunity to ask; "Anne, just what is an art camp? That's something new to me."

"My friend Barbara actually manages the Shoreside Art Camp that Nancy is attending. They conduct classes in a wide variety of topics during the summer and Nancy is taking the three week photography workshop they offer. The art camp has somewhat basic accommodations so Nancy decided to stay here at the Inn."

I didn't know much about Nancy but her abrupt departure after that phone call had me puzzled and somewhat concerned. My concern increased over the next few days as Nancy neither returned nor called Barbara or Anne. Nancy had simply disappeared.

# # #

Anne was always friendly at breakfast and during her brief visits to the Inn's living room in the evenings. I would take these opportunities to discuss events in the community and to ask about Nancy. I enjoyed these brief visits with Anne and she helped me understand more about this small coastal town that depended on lobster fishing rather than tourism for economic survival.

I should also mention that I would occasionally encounter Anne out in the community but her warm personality at the Inn was very professional when we saw one another on the street or in a shop. I was acknowledged as "Mr. Wilson" if any greeting even occurred.

At breakfast on Wednesday Anne responded to my inquiry about Nancy by saying;

"Barbara and I have not received a response from our calls to Nancy. I have also called the college and left a message for Nancy to please call me when she returns."

Anne added; "Barbara and I are both puzzled by her abrupt departure but Nancy certainly has no obligation to report her reason for leaving to us."

I speculated; "I still assume from her reaction that morning that she received some bad news, possibly some type of family emergency."

On Friday Anne indicated, "Nancy's workshop is scheduled to end tomorrow. If I don't hear anything by then I will just pack up her belongings and have Sally make the room available as scheduled for our next guests."

At breakfast on Saturday Anne told me she still had not heard from Nancy so she had packed Nancy's belongings and Sally was cleaning the room so it would be ready for the new guests.

After breakfast I said to Anne;

"I'm getting concerned about Nancy's reaction to that phone call and I would like to try my luck at contacting her but I don't have her contact information."

Anne replied; "No problem, let's take a look at her registration card in the office."

I took that opportunity to use my cell phone to take a photo of the registration card that Anne had on file for Nancy at the front desk. Nancy's registration card, like mine, contained cell phone number, email address, auto tag and her home address.

5

4th Week of August

As the last week of August began, I was making some progress with my book but my attention had been diverted by the recent events in Stone Harbor. Admittedly, I am curious by nature and was now distracted by the new mystery surrounding Nancy's missing photos and her sudden departure.

I had done an online search on Sunday morning and confirmed a Nancy Olson was associated with the college in her hometown and her academic profile indicated she had a degree in both history and art. Interesting, Nancy was actually a history professor at the college so it appeared that her summer photography workshop was a hobby.

Nancy's scheduled workshop had ended over the past weekend so on Monday morning I decided to call the college in Missouri and ask to speak to her. My call was transferred to a recorded message;

"Please leave a message. Miss Olson will be available when classes start in September."

The college website indicated classes were scheduled to begin the following week. So, I decided to wait until classes started the following week to try to contact Nancy again. I wanted to tell her I had her iPad as I was certain she would like to have it returned. Nancy's other belongings had been put in storage and the room was now occupied by a couple from Florida.

By now I had become seriously distracted by the events unfolding in Stone Harbor. My inquisitive nature was taking over. Rob's death and the possibility of a lobster war provided an excuse for me to learn more about lobstermen and lobster fishing.

Maine Lobster Boat at Work

I recalled seeing an advertisement for day trips on a lobster boat during my earlier visits to Portland and Boothbay. An online search found several such "educational" trips aboard a lobster boat in a nearby town that catered to tourists. I made a call and booked a trip for the following day. This turned out to be a fun and educational experience.

#   #   #

I arrived early for my educational tour and took the opportunity to take my morning walk and explore the nearby community. I was pleased to discover that the local book store was open and that it also served coffee and had a display for pastry. I was intrigued by their collection on old maps and nautical charts and purchased a couple for my collection.

The lobster boat departed the dock later Tuesday morning with two couples and me aboard. The captain explained the basics of lobster fishing on our voyage out of the harbor. He also said that each of us would have the opportunity to pick up a lobster buoy and learn how to unload a few lobsters from a lobster trap.

The Captain announced; "First of all you need to know how to pronounce their name, it's a lobstah, not lobster. The lobstahmen also call lobstahs a bug, so when you hear conversations around the docks about bugs they are talking about lobstahs."

"When you boarded our lobster boat you probably noticed the pile of lobster traps near the dock. That's the type of lobster trap you will be working with today."

Lobster Traps

"Maine has almost 6,000 licensed commercial lobstermen who are authorized to have up to 800 traps or pots per lobster boat. A lobsterman is licensed to fish in one of seven zones and the lobsterman may set traps anywhere within the authorized zone."

"An apprenticeship is required to even qualify for a license and there is a long waiting list. It can take years to even get a new license. However, Maine has made provisions to help a son or daughter keep a license in the family to help preserve the family nature of the lobster business."

"Every lobster boat has a unique buoy to mark the location of its traps and must display one of those buoys on the cabin top of their boat. Notice the buoy on top of our boat and the different colors and designs of the buoys you see all around you."

"A special tool is used to measure each lobster from the rear of the eye socket to the rear of the carapace. Only the carapace, the main body, not the tail is measured. Lobstermen may only keep a lobster that measures more than 3 1/4 inches and less than 5 inches. All other lobsters in their traps must be returned to the sea."

"A lobster boat may not keep a female lobster with eggs and must cut a V notch in the breeding female's tail. We are not permitted to keep any female lobster with a V notch."

"Lobster boats are typically owned by the captain who must also hold the license. The captain will hire a mate called a sternman to pull the traps, empty and sort the lobster, bait and return the trap to the water."

"Lobstermen are paid when they unload their lobster and sell their catch at the dock. The sternman will receive approximately 20% of what they get paid for that day's catch."

"It is unlawful for anyone but the licensed owner to raise or molest any lobster trap without permission from a state representative."

"The captain navigates and runs the boat using a combination of local knowledge and GPS to locate his lobster buoys. GPS is useful on foggy days as the lobstermen work traps everyday but Sunday."

"The sternman's job is to hook the lobster buoy with a hooked pole, pick up the line, place the line in the hydraulic winch and raise the lobster trap up to the rail of the boat, open the trap, remove any lobsters, sort the lobsters, bait the trap and place it back in the water."

Lobster Trap on Lobster Boat Rail

"Each of you will have the opportunity to raise a trap today and do the job of a sternman."

"After you inspect the lobster for eggs you will measure it to make certain it's a keeper. You will then use this tool to place the rubber bands on the claws and place the lobster in this holding tank with circulating sea water."

He pointed to a grey container about the size of a large suitcase.

"This is your bait tote. After you pull the trap and remove the lobsters you will need to place more bait in the trap before you push it back in the water."

"If we were going to sell the lobsters we pick up today we would place them in a lobster crate like this one when we arrive at the dock."

"You will notice these crates have vents on the side and if placed in the water the crates will float. Lobsters can be kept alive in this type of crate while waiting to be picked up by a truck for delivery to a distributor."

"Lobstermen tend to go out at sunrise and and return to the town dock in the afternoon to weigh and sell their catch at the local lobster dock."

I had observed this activity from the Fisherman's deck as the town dock was nearby and the dinghy dock was just below the Fisherman's deck. That location obviously made it very convenient for some of the lobstermen to stop for something to eat and drink at the Pub before they drove home.

Lobstermen may start early each day when the weather tends to be calmest but, as I had already observed, they actually go out to empty their traps in all kinds of nasty weather.

The trip on the lobster boat gave me the opportunity to ask the Captain a number of questions toward the end of our trip.

"Does a captain always have a sternman or do some captains work alone?"

"It's hard work and unusual to see a captain work alone but for some reason a few seem to do it. I think it's generally just when they can't get a sternman that day."

"How often does someone get their boot caught in a lobster buoy line when they toss the trap overboard?"

"It's really rare, these guys know to be careful. When it does happen they generally bang their leg on the side of the boat. However, I heard someone got pulled overboard and drowned recently at Stone Harbor. Stupid accident."

"How does a captain decide where to place his

lobster traps? I see buoys of all different colors around this boat."

"They all have their favorite locations based on experience. The lobster boats in each community tend to work nearby and you will see different colored buoys mixed together. In some places it seems you could almost step from buoy to buoy."

"Do disputes ever happen between groups of lobstermen about fishing in waters they consider their local fishing grounds?"

"Yea, that happens from time-to-time. These are strong, independent people that feel they have a right to protect their local fishing grounds from outsiders."

"Finally, I have heard someone talk about lobster boat races. What's a lobster boat race?"

"Lobster fishing is hard work. The lobstermen started racing their boats to have some fun. It's now a serious competitive weekend."

#   #   #

When I returned to the Inn Tuesday evening, Anne was visiting with the other guests in the living room. I was pleased when she asked me about my adventure on the lobster boat. It had been an enjoyable day for this city boy and I was happy to share the experience with her.

Anne apparently knew little about lobster fishing and asked a lot of questions and I was happy to sound like an expert. Anne was a good listener and we talked about my experience much longer than I would have anticipated.

I also mentioned; "Our family in Kentucky had a small sailboat on one of the Kentucky lakes. Sailing was a frequent activity when I was a teenager on summer weekends. I enjoyed that voyage on the lobster boat yesterday and it got me thinking about adding boating to my retirement plan."

Anne then said; "Thanks for telling me about your adventure. I don't know much about lobster fishing but I actually own a lobster boat."

"My husband and I bought it after he retired and we moved to Stone Harbor. I decided to keep it after he died and my friend Barbara and I still enjoy a day on the water."

I was puzzled and replied; "You actually own a lobster boat? Is it used for lobster fishing?"

Anne answered; "Oh no, some people call them lobster yachts; it has a very nice cabin."

"Barbara and I actually used my boat with Nancy's workshop. You might have noticed some of Nancy's photos were taken while out on the water. The days you've seen Sam the cook serving breakfast are the days that Barbara and I have gone out on my boat with one of her workshop classes."

6

Wednesday marked eleven days after Nancy's abrupt departure. I again began thinking about Nancy's missing photos as the librarian had told me she had no clue why they were gone. Why would anybody want to remove three of Nancy's photos?

I still had Nancy's iPad sitting on the dresser. I had no justification for snooping and was concerned about invading her privacy. My years in the banking business working with both bank regulators and law enforcement agencies had taught me to respect the laws and regulations covering customer confidentiality. Opening Nancy's iPad would certainly violate her right to privacy.

However, my concern had increased by the day and I wanted to look at the missing photos again. My career had advanced because I not only have a memory for numbers but I can recall unique number sequences and relationships. That talent had served me well as an auditor investigating illegal financial activity.

Nancy had used her personal code to open her iPad the day we reviewed her photos while standing outside the library. I had watched her enter her code that day and would have no problem recalling it if I decided to open her iPad.

If I opened her iPad I could then look for the photos that had been on display at the library. I convinced myself it would not be an invasion of her privacy if I just looked at the photos she had already shown me. So I entered her code, the iPad opened and I began reviewing her photos.

Nancy's photos were all neatly organized in specific files by topic and I quickly located her file for the workshop with sub-files for birds, landscapes, and boats. I opened the workshop file and then opened the boat photo file. She also had a sub-file for final lobster boat photos and I recalled that was the file she showed me on the day we reviewed her photos at the library.

As a result, it was fairly easy for me to narrow down my search and identify the photos that had been on display at the library. The three missing photos were part of a sequence of several dozen photos taken from a distance and showed two men on a small floating dock loading gear on a lobster boat early in the morning.

Two of the missing photos were close-ups of the two men working on the dock and then on the boat when it headed out to sea. Other photos in the sequence were wide-angle views of the same scene.

So what was so special about these three photos that were missing? Nothing looked unusual to me. Why had they mysteriously disappeared?

I remained puzzled, closed the iPad and went to bed.

#   #   #

I awoke Thursday morning thinking about numbers - working lobster boats have large, visible registration numbers. I reopened Nancy's iPad to examine the numbers on the boat in the missing photos. I then did an online search of boat ownership in Maine and discovered the photos were taken of a boat owned by Robert James in Stone Harbor. Rob's boat?

Nancy's photos were also all time and date stamped and further investigation indicated they were actually taken the night before Rob died. The photos were not taken in the morning as I had assumed.

I next reviewed the entire sequence of several dozen photos and it suddenly occurred to me the importance of what I was seeing - two men were loading bait totes on Rob's boat and both men departed with four bait totes onboard - Rob was not alone when he departed his dock that night.

I also noted that two pickups were parked next to the dock. Based on the comments at the Pub, I assumed the silver pickup belonged to Rob and that the black pickup belonged to the second man. The sequence of photos indicated that several of the bait totes had been loaded on the boat from the black pickup.

It occurred to me that just because Rob's deserted boat was discovered the following morning, it did not necessarily mean Rob had actually departed alone that morning. How could I find out if Rob and this second man had returned to Rob's dock later that night and then Rob departed alone the next morning?

The Portland and Bangor newspapers had published photos of Rob's lobster boat after it was towed back to the town dock and I searched online for these back issues. The photos in the newspapers confirmed this was the same boat and I noticed that it appeared that only two of the bait totes remained on Rob's boat. The newspaper articles also had a photo of Rob.

I returned to Nancy's iPad and examined the close-up photos in more detail. The quality of Nancy's color photos was really amazing and, even though taken at a distance, I could now clearly identify

Rob and see that the second man had red hair.

Now what? How do I explain what I have discovered on Nancy's iPad? Who is the man with red hair and why was he with Rob on his boat that night? When and where did this second man get off Rob's boat? What happened to the other two bait totes?

I copied the photos Nancy had taken the night before Rob's death and the articles from the newspapers to my laptop and cell phone so I would have them available if needed.

#   #   #

The Medical Examiner's reports for both Rob's and Mary Alice's deaths were released later that day:

"Mary Alice James died of an overdose of fentanyl. An excessive amount of fentanyl was found in her body and her fingerprints were found on the syringe located next to her body. Both of her arms showed signs of needle tracks."

"Robert James died as a result of a blow to his head and only an insignificant amount of water was found in his lungs. This would indicate he may still have been alive when he entered the water but unconscious and not able to save himself. The evidence provided indicated the deceased had been pulled overboard by a lobster trap buoy line wrapped around his boot. The deceased had no other injuries or traces of illegal drugs in his body."

#   #   #

The news traveled fast and Sandy had a busy day at the cafe on Friday.

"It's just sad about Mary Alice. Nice girl, Kathy and I went to school with her. Never would have guessed she would die of an overdose."

"Don't say I told you but Kathy told me Mary Alice was looking for a new source of drugs down at the Pub. Her brother Dave thinks that Rob was the one been getting heroin for her."

"Don't think I want to know how she got her hands on that fentanyl. Must have been desperate to shoot that much into her arm and overdose."

"Strange if Rob was her source why he didn't have traces of drugs in his body."

"Wonder how he hit his head on the boat? The guys at the Pub think it might have been a fight with some boat from the island."

Sandy was right - conversations at the Pub that afternoon all focused on the Medical Examiner's report's conclusion that Rob's head injury caused his death.

"Damn fool report; they can't explain how Rob hit his head and didn't hit his legs when he was pulled overboard. Just doesn't make sense."

"Boy didn't drown. Looks to me like somebody must'a hit him on the head then put that line around his boot!"

Captain Peggy said; "Slow down; working alone he could have hit his head on almost anything and tripped or fallen, got his foot caught in the line and knocked that trap overboard."

Max concluded; "Damn shame. Hard tellin' what happened and no way to prove anything."

#   #   #

I didn't want to disclose what I had discovered on Nancy's iPad until I knew whom to trust. I was uncomfortable disclosing that I even had Nancy's iPad and had violated her privacy by opening it to examine her photos. I also was uncertain if I wanted anyone to know I had copies of the photos that had been removed from the library exhibit as I now suspected someone didn't want those photos to be in circulation.

My trip on the lobster boat had given me an opportunity to ask a number of questions and although I had learned it is unusual, a number of lobstermen would work alone.

I try to pay attention to details and I had noted four bait totes with their covers attached in Nancy's photos but thought it unusual that two of those totes appeared to be taped shut. However, newspaper photos indicated only the two bait totes without tape remained aboard after Rob's boat had been towed to the town dock. Neither Nancy's photos nor the newspaper photos showed any lobster crates for live lobsters.

Was there any reason a lobster boat would return with fewer bait totes than when the boat departed the dock?

Our Captain on my lobster boat tour had been very polite and helpful and I had asked if it was OK if I called him if I had any followup questions. He had said yes, so I called him;

"What happens to the bait totes after they are empty? Is there any reason you would not return them to the dock?"

He obviously considered my question to be from a stupid tourist and replied; "Of course not, where would they go? We don't pollute our fishing waters by throwing crap overboard."

My short voyage on the lobster boat had been fun, educational and very informative. I was now even more curious about what might have been in the two other totes loaded onto Rob's boat that night and what had happened to them.

I considered what I had learned and now suspected Nancy's photos of Rob's boat, of the second man with red hair, of the missing bait totes and Nancy's sudden departure were all connected. Was it possible the second man had something to do with Rob's death?

7

1st Week of September

It was now the first week of September so I called the college again on Monday morning since classes were scheduled to start that day and Nancy should be back on campus. Once again I was transferred to her office and listened to a new message.

"On a temporary basis Miss Olson's classes will be conducted by Mrs. Alexander."

#   #   #

Nancy had now been gone for two weeks with no contact. Anne had told me that morning that Nancy still had not responded to any of the messages from Barbara or her. In any event, neither Anne nor Barbara thought it was appropriate for them to file a missing persons report with the sheriff's office.

I felt I had violated Nancy's privacy by opening her iPad and did not share this information with Anne or Barbara. At this point, I don't even recall if I had told anyone that Nancy had forgotten her iPad the morning she departed so abruptly. I was now concerned Nancy might be in danger.

By now thoughts of working on my novel were replaced by the mystery related to Rob's death, Nancy's missing photos, my growing concern about Nancy's reaction to the mysterious phone call and her rapid departure.

During the past week I had continued my normal daily routine of a morning walk, breakfast at the Inn, working on my novel on the Fisherman's deck, lunch at the local cafe and sitting on the Fishermen's deck to enjoy an afternoon beer. My concern for Nancy had increased as each day went by without a response to my message at the college.

I walked over to the deck, opened my laptop and started reviewing online information about Nancy. My fraud and money laundering investigations in the past had required me to analyze a wide variety of computer and online systems including information on the dark web.

Few people appreciate how much personal information they post about themselves on social media is easily obtainable. In addition, a treasure trove of personal data is easily available online from government websites.

The usual pubic information about Nancy was quickly located and downloaded to a file on my laptop. Nancy owned a small house near the college, owned her late model car, graduated from a state college and had earned her doctorate in history from a private college. She had been married, divorced and had obtained a restraining order against her husband during their divorce.

However, I was frustrated by the absence of social media accounts as that's frequently the best source of personal information about someone's friends, trips and their location at any point in time.

My curiosity about the contents of her iPad had steadily increased and I decided it was now important to examine more of its contents. I had it with me and opened it again.

Nancy apparently utilized the normal apps for phone, email, text, maps, weather and news. However, as I expected, she had no social media apps on her iPad so very limited personal information was available. I could locate no information about family or friends.

Her digital books were well organized into folders for history, art, travel guides for Maine and academic papers for her college. Further examination of her photo folders revealed numerous files of photos grouped by topics; birds, boats, places and groups of people. I could locate a few photos of individuals but no files were established for friends or family.

Nancy did have the "Find My iPhone" app installed but this required me to have her password to open it. If I had her password I could locate her phone on the device's map and hopefully locate Nancy but this was impossible without her password.

I didn't understand why she was not responding to the messages from Anne and Barbara. I recognized we were only briefly acquainted but saw no reason she would ignore their inquires.

8

My concern for Nancy's safety had intensified after I learned Nancy had not returned to her college. I still felt somewhat guilty looking through the files in Nancy's iPad but at this stage I decided it was essential that I try to locate Nancy and continued my review of her iPad that afternoon.

I was frustrated by the absence of any social media apps. Nancy had no Facebook or LinkedIn contacts. My review of her iPad indicated she was methodical with text and email and deleted most messages after they were read.

So my next action was to start reviewing the deleted items in her trash. This search also proved equally frustrating as Nancy was very private and careful and it appeared she would periodically empty her trash files. Her trash file contained mostly news updates but three recent emails proved to be interesting.

The first email said; "Jane, I will see you tomorrow."

Nancy had written an email to the college saying she planned to return late because of a "family emergency" and would keep them posted.

The final email of interest was from a obscure email address that simply stated; "I want those photos and your camera - tell me where to meet you".

I thought about emailing Jane but decided it was best to wait until I learned more as Nancy apparently wanted to remain out of sight. I was certainly developing more questions than answers at this stage. How did the person contacting Nancy even know her personal cell phone number and email address? Was this the same person that had called her the morning she departed so abruptly?

The good news was the email deletions clearly meant Nancy had access to the Internet and had not been located. The bad news was I suspected someone was looking for her and probably wanted to destroy those incriminating photos. If that person was responsible for Rob's death then Nancy could be in real danger.

I needed Nancy's password to open her Find My iPhone app in order to locate her. I had never observed her opening her laptop or entering other passwords so my power of observation was useless. Both her "Notes" and "Reminders" apps were blank - no password information.

This woman was incredibly private and careful - if she even risked hiding her passwords where would she hide them? The only documents I could identify were contained in her iBooks app. So that night after dinner I began a careful review of each of the hundreds of documents listed. No luck after several frustrating hours of reviewing mostly academic papers.

It was late and because I was exhausted and frustrated, I went to bed.

# # #

On Tuesday morning I took my morning walk, then joined the other guests for breakfast and adjourned to the Fisherman's deck as usual. Once again I had my notebook, my laptop and this morning I again took Nancy's iPad with me to my table on the deck.

I had only examined Nancy's workshop photo file in my earlier review. I started reviewing Nancy's other photo files and as expected, given the thousands of photos, this was a very tedious process. I continued to admire her work - a very talented photographer.

As time passed, my scanning of her photos accelerated. If Nancy had used an image to save her passwords I was unable to locate it. So, how could I locate Nancy?

I was embarrassed to admit that I had been overlooking an obvious answer to my question. Most of Nancy's photos had time, date and location noted with each photo but the iPad application I had been reviewing only noted the time and date on each photo. I had only been focused on her older photos but I had also discovered she had been adding photos to her files during the past week.

Those newer photos were again of birds and landscapes and I had only noted time and date, as a result, they gave me no clue to her location so I had simply been ignoring them. Nancy's iPad photo program also had the "Places" feature and when I clicked this icon it opened a map of the United States that illustrated where her photos had been taken.

Nancy had thousands of photos on her iPad and the groups of photos on the map were very general. If I could locate her most recent photos I might have a clue to her whereabouts. So I began another tedious search and I started clicking on the files with fewer photos to review.

After an hour or so I located the most recent group of photos in an area of North Carolina noted as "Wilderness". Even zooming in on the map did not reveal much additional information. The photos had been taken in a variety of areas up in the North Carolina mountains so I had only a general idea where Nancy might be staying. I also discovered several new photos had been taken earlier that morning from the same general location. Why was she in North Carolina? Why had Nancy not returned to teach her class?

My curiosity and concern got the best of me. I decided it was now time for me to try and find Nancy so I booked a flight from Bangor to Charlotte for Wednesday morning.

9

Wednesday morning I packed a travel bag and planned to depart after breakfast. I didn't like misleading Anne but I still didn't know what information to share or whom to trust.

"Anne, I need to go back to New York and I will come back to the Inn in a few days. This is proving to be a great location to work on my novel."

I was surprised when Anne replied;

"No problem. By the way, I got a text from Nancy last night. She apologized for not responding sooner but said she had been focused on a family emergency and not to worry. She also said not to worry about the few belongings she left behind as nothing was important."

I was relieved that Anne had now heard from Nancy but very surprised Nancy did not mention her lost iPad. Anne's information did not change my plans and I drove to the Bangor airport in my rental car after breakfast.

Anne's news had me somewhat confused - was that text really from Nancy or had something happened? Why didn't she ask about her iPad? Why didn't Nancy return to teach her class at the college? Why communicate now?

The drive to Bangor and a aircraft mechanical issue delayed my arrival in Charlotte until later that day. I picked up my new rental car and once again activated the iPad photo app and confirmed that several new photos had been added that day in the same "Wilderness" location. I headed west on the Interstate highways toward Asheville and the general location of "Wilderness".

Darkness interrupted my journey so I pulled off the Interstate onto a two-lane highway and stopped at a local motel as I neared the general area of Nancy's photos.

#   #   #

Thursday morning I grabbed a quick breakfast at the motel's breakfast counter, checked out and resumed driving down the two-lane highway toward Nancy's location.

As I neared the area where Nancy had taken her photos, I saw a small sign along the highway next to a narrow paved road: "Wilderness Art Colony". Of course, Nancy felt safest with her fellow artists in a remote art camp!

I drove a few miles up to the camp and was not disappointed. It was the rustic remote facility I had envisioned. I assumed the numerous small buildings that were scattered in the woods around the property were for housing and classrooms.

It was now midmorning. I parked with some other cars and looked for a building that might be an office. As I neared what I thought to be an office I spotted Nancy walking out of an adjoining building and she simultaneously spotted me.

Nancy's reaction was one of fright and she quickly disappeared behind the building. She had been walking and talking with another woman who was clearly confused as Nancy had not said a word, just disappeared.

I approached the other woman and introduced myself.

"Hi, I'm Steve Wilson are you Jane?"

"Yes" with a surprised look.

"It's really important I talk to Nancy. I have some important personal information to share with her. Would you please ask her to talk to me."

Jane responded; "OK, I will ask her" and gave me a suspicious look as she walked away.

Jane went in search of Nancy and a short while later Nancy reluctantly reappeared but insisted we sit out in the open at a picnic table in full view of the other students. I took out Nancy's iPad and, to her surprise, opened it.

"Nancy, I think these are the photos that were removed from the library, is that correct?"

"Yes, they were part of a series I submitted to my workshop."

"At first I thought these photos were taken early in the morning, but the time stamp indicates they were taken at night. Correct?"

"Yes, I generally took photos of the lobster boats in the morning as they started their day. I would sometimes stop to take photos in the evening on my way back to the Inn and I just happened to see some activity on that boat that night and took the photos."

"Do you know anything about that boat?"

"No, why?"

"Do you remember the deserted lobster boat and the body they discovered the weekend before you departed Stone Harbor?"

"Yes, why?"

"That's the boat that belonged to Rob, the dead lobsterman that was found with a buoy line wrapped around his boot."

"So?"

"Your photos show a second man departed on the boat with Rob that night. Rob was presumed to have departed alone on his boat the following morning. I don't know if Rob returned home that night, and if not, then I suspect that second man might have something to do with Rob's death and removing your photos."

I also reminded Nancy about the visit by Mary Alice to the Pub and her death by a drug overdose.

"Mary Alice told the deputy sheriff that she thought Rob had gone to his boat early the next morning as usual before she got up. But I think it's strange that she made no mention of Rob going out the night before."

"Nancy, I have not discussed either your photos or my suspicions about the second man with anyone as I thought it most important to locate you first. I don't really have confidence in the local deputy sheriff as he seemed more than willing to quickly accept both deaths as accidental."

"So let me ask you - what was that phone call about and why did you depart so abruptly?"

Nancy said a male voice had said, "Nancy, your photos are fantastic. We want to buy all of your Maine photos. We can meet you at the old house about a mile down the road from the art camp. Just name your price."

"At first I was complemented but the tone of his voice, the fact that he didn't identify himself, the unusual meeting location and the name your price comment just didn't sound right. I was surprised and then when I thought about the missing photos I got frightened and just left town and kept driving."

"I drove my own car to Maine so I had no need to worry about a rental car and the stuff I left behind was not that important. I just didn't know what to do or where to go. I was afraid my photos had revealed something that man didn't want to be seen. I just wanted to disappear."

"The first couple of days I just stayed in a motel in Vermont trying to decide what I should do and where to go. Each day I received at least one call on my cell phone, a text message or an email that became more threatening. I was afraid to return home and decided I would be safest here at the art colony so I called my friend Jane."

"Jane and I have been friends for many years and have both attended this art colony in the past. I know the owner and we had no problem arranging for me to stay and take a photography class."

"Why didn't you return any calls from Anne or Barbara?"

"I don't really know Anne or Barbara and had no idea what this was about or who might be involved. I decided to tell both Barbara and Anne a few days ago that it was a family emergency so they would stop trying to contact me."

"I don't really know you either and I was concerned since the photos disappeared after we went to the library together. I just decided not to trust anyone."

As she began to relax she finally asked; "How did you find me?"

"Well, first I told Anne I was concerned about that phone call you received and I wanted to try and contact you. To do so I needed your contact information, so about a week ago Anne and I went to her office and I took a photo of your registration card. I looked you up online, called the college and left you a message."

"I called the college again on Monday and learned you had not returned to teach your classes. As a result, my concern for your welfare increased."

"In addition, as you can see, I have your iPad. You

left it behind on the deck the day you got that call and departed so abruptly. I find it easy to remember numbers and I could recall the code you used to open your iPad that day at the library."

"I was concerned about invading your privacy but you had let me view your photos so I decided it was OK to view your photo files again. I had begun to suspect the missing photos were connected to your sudden departure. I was then able to use your iPad map and the location information from your recent photos to find you."

Nancy asked me; "How do you think that caller got my contact information? I try to be very careful with my personal information but he knows both my cell phone number and my email address! That makes me angry and scares me!"

"I don't know - that's a very good question since I certainly couldn't find that information online. If we assume your caller is someone in Stone Harbor, then it might have been a local source. Other than the Inn, did you provide that information to anyone else in Stone Harbor?"

"Yes, I think the registration card I completed at the art camp has all the same information."

"Well it was certainly possible for someone to walk in and get your contact information from one of those registration cards like I did."

We visited for several hours and shared everything we knew about recent events. I learned the caller left strange messages that had threatened to harm her family.

"Be a shame if anything happened to your family while you were away so it's important that you answer my next call."

Nancy told me she was an only child and her parents had both died several years earlier. She had been married but was now divorced with no children. Threats to her family were therefore meaningless and she had not responded.

I advised; "Nancy, you should keep all future messages on your phone so you can share them with the authorities in the future."

I then asked; "Why are you so very careful with your personal information?"

Nancy replied; "When I was divorced several years ago, my ex-husband became very possessive and would not stop calling me. So I changed all my contact information and got a restraining order. That's all stopped but I just decided to remain very careful."

"I called that same attorney to ask about a new restraining order for these calls. But he told me that would be a waste of time if I didn't know the name or location of my caller."

We decided she was indeed safest at the art colony and I told her I would find a motel and contact Mark Bouchard, one of my friends that worked at the FBI, for advice. Mark lived and worked in New York and we had worked on some very complex cases together. I trusted his judgement and we had become both professional and personal friends.

# # #

I located another nearby local motel, booked a room for Thursday night and called Mark. I briefed him on everything I had learned and asked his advice.

I was disappointed but not surprised when Mark responded;

"Steve, this is all very interesting and I am personally concerned for Nancy's safety. I would like to help but you have provided insufficient evidence for our agency or any other federal agency to initiate an investigation. As of now this would be a matter for the local authorities."

The fact that Nancy was receiving frequent threats convinced me that she was in serious trouble. Rob was not alone on his boat that night and the Medical Examiner had concluded the cause of death was related to the gash on his head. Was

Rob's death really an accident or had someone killed him and staged the buoy line around his boot as a cover up? Did Rob die that night or the next morning? In my opinion, Nancy's photos could incriminate that second man in a possible murder.

I had overheard the lobstermen say that Rob's boat had been searched for drugs on several occasions but that none were ever discovered. If drugs were not involved then what was so important that Rob would end up dead?

#   #   #

Nancy had agreed I could keep her iPad that night so I sat down and looked carefully at the photos. I again saw that two men were loading bait totes onto Rob's boat and again confirmed that there were four bait totes on the aft deck when they departed Rob's dock that night. The newspaper photos indicated only two bait totes remained on Rob's boat when it was towed to the town dock. What had happened to the other two bait totes?

Obviously something had gone wrong since Rob was now dead and Nancy was being threatened. Nancy's photos were the key to this puzzle. How do I convince the FBI or DEA to get involved?

I had a long history of working with the FBI, DEA and other federal agencies concerning fraud and money laundering. They would take any evidence I provided seriously but I no longer had the resources available to me that I had when I worked behind a desk at the bank. I had no experience as a field investigator and at this stage had no real evidence that the second man was involved in anything illegal. I was now on my own and decided I needed to return to Stone Harbor to investigate.

Convinced that Nancy was safe at the moment, I decided to return to Stone Harbor on Friday to see what I might learn that would be helpful. I was never a detective and very uncertain how to proceed. My only sources of information had been listening to local gossip from Sandy at the cafe, eavesdropping on conversations at the Pub and possibly getting additional information about Stone Harbor from Anne.

I drove to Charlotte on Friday morning, turned in my rental car and took a flight back to Bangor. When I returned to the Inn later that afternoon I was greeted by Anne.

"How was your trip to New York? Get everything done?"

"Yes, everything back in order, no problem. Thanks for asking."

10

The lobster boat races were scheduled for that weekend in Stone Harbor and the town was packed with participants and spectators when I returned Friday afternoon. Fisherman's was packed to overflowing with a very boisterous crowd. Thankfully, I was now considered a "regular" at Fisherman's and Kathy managed to get me a small table for dinner in the dining room.

I was tired from my trip but stayed for a short while to participate in my new favorite activity - eavesdropping. It was evident that both lobster boat drivers and their supporters from a wide variety of coastal communities were in town to participate in the weekend races. It was quickly apparent to me that these races were serious, competitive fun.

I recognized Captain Max's voice at a table in the dining room. This was really the first time I could match the voice with the man standing next to a boisterous table. His appearance matched my expectation; Max was a stocky six feet with grey hair matched by a short grey beard. Max just looked the part of a tough lobsterman.

Max apparently took these lobster racing events very seriously and I overheard one of the other local lobstermen asking if he had found time to put his special racing engine in his boat.

Max responded; "Damn right, can't let one of those island boats beat me!"

Hundreds of lobstermen and their supporters, including several boats from the nearby island, were in Stone Harbor for the races. I overheard an undercurrent of tension at Fisherman's that night. Rumors of a potential conflict between the lobstermen in Stone Harbor and the lobstermen from the island were circulating throughout the restaurant. Everyone seemed to know about the dispute over fishing areas and the local suspicions related to Rob's death.

It also appeared the local crowd was frustrated that the local deputy sheriff was not pursuing a possible link between the island boats and Rob's death.

"Damn deputy is too lazy or scared to question the lobstermen from the island."

#   #   #

When I returned to the Inn I decided to do some quick research on lobster boat races before I went to bed. The first thing I discovered was these seemingly informal races had an official organization called the Maine Lobster Boat Racing Association.

An article in the Bangor Daily News described the races to date with descriptions of the winning boats. Power & Motoryacht magazine also had an article that described a previous event in Boothbay Harbor.

Lobster Boat Race @ Bangor Daily News

I learned that lobster boat races are conducted each summer with events in about a dozen waterfront towns. This weekend's race in Stone Harbor was the last event of the season. Most of the races are divided into classes based on boat size and engine horsepower. The major event over the weekend would be the unlimited race that would determine the fastest boat.

What I overheard at Fisherman's was confirmed by the articles I read about previous events. Most of the boats are actual lobster boats used for fishing but some of the owners modify their engines just for the races. There is an 'anything goes' attitude to gain an advantage that would win first place.

Lobster fishing is a tough business and these racing weekends are an excuse for lobstermen to cut loose with friends and family and have some fun. Their family and friends join in for an exciting weekend together.

The entertainment starts when most of the boats show up the night before racing day and the party starts. Towns like Stone Harbor don't have accommodations for such a large crowd and most of the participants drink beer with their supporters and spend the night on their boats.

#   #   #

It was a very exciting weekend. Anne joined me on the deck at Fisherman's to watch the action. The harbor was packed with lobster boats. There was standing room only on the Fisherman's deck for family, friends and visitors along the waterfront and on the moored boats in the harbor.

A path had been cleared through the harbor for the racing boats and the races began with incredible noise from both the crowds and some of the modified boat engines.

Not many women enter these races so the local crowd was very excited when Captain Peggy won her class. Peggy was a sharp contrast to Max. She was tall and slender with flowing dark hair. Her victory was clearly a matter of local pride and Captain Peggy was now a local hero!

The local crowd was equally excited when Max won the unlimited race in a very close finish with one of the island boats. The trouble started when Max was accused of cheating by the driver of the island boat when they returned to the town dock for the awards ceremony.

Accusing Max of cheating in front of the home crowd nearly started a riot. Fortunately, the deputy was nearby and he confined the situation to name calling and some pushing and shoving.

The driver of the island boat angrily departed with;

"Stay out of our fishing grounds if you know what's good for you!"

Max shouted in return;

"I will fish where I damn well please. Fuck you!"

The likelihood that a lobster war could explode in the coming weeks was apparent to everyone that overheard their hostile exchange.

11

As I started what was originally intended to be my sixth and last week at the Inn, I wanted for all appearances to resume my usual daily pattern. I thought it best to extend my stay so I could further investigate my suspicions. On Monday morning after breakfast I asked:

"Anne, I am making steady progress on my novel and the Inn is working out better than I expected. Would it be possible to stay a couple of extra weeks?"

"Let me check my books. It's a busy time of year but I am certain I can make arrangements. I enjoy having you as a guest."

# # #

After breakfast I had decided that if my suspicions about the second man were correct, then I might be withholding evidence. I may not have had confidence in the local deputy sheriff but I had an obligation to share Nancy's photos, so I arranged to meet him later that morning at the town hall.

The local deputy appeared to be in his mid-thirties and I wondered if he had enough experience to deal with a possible murder investigation.

"Sheriff, these are the photos that someone removed several weeks ago from the display at the library. These photos of Rob's boat were taken by Nancy Olson the night before his deserted boat was discovered. You will notice that Rob and the other man departed on the boat together. Rob was not alone that night."

The deputy sheriff responded; "How do you know they both didn't return to Rob's dock later that night?"

"I don't, but when you spoke to Mary Alice did she mention that Rob departed on his boat that night?"

"I didn't ask her that question and I can't ask her now. Assume you know she died of a drug overdose."

"Don't you think is worthwhile to ask that man with Rob about what happened that night?"

"I don't know or recognize that guy. If I do see him I will ask him. Thanks for sharing the photos."

"Sheriff, I really think this could be important."

"Listen, mister, you are a stranger and know nothing about this lobster business. I got a war about to start and me and the deputy for that island got our hands full."

I was frustrated and disappointed when I departed the deputy's office. I had shared my concerns with no meaningful response. It looked like the lobstermen's opinion of their local deputy was right; he apparently was not really interested in making an effort to solve a potential crime.

I certainly didn't know Max but based on what I had overheard at both the Pub and the Lobster Boat Races, I had no doubt he and his friends would start placing traps in the disputed area.

The local deputy viewed me as an outsider with a couple of photos that I thought might be important. But, he might be right. What if my suspicions were wrong and Rob had returned home that night and just had an unfortunate accident the next morning. But I remained curious - what were they doing that night and what happened to the other two bait totes?

On the other hand, Rob could have had an argument with an island lobsterman and his alleged accident could have been a cover up. In either case, the second man in Nancy's photos would have had nothing to do with Rob's death.

When I returned to my room at the Inn I decided to do a little research on local law enforcement. I confirmed that Stone Harbor was too small to have it's own police department and relied on the county sheriff's office for law enforcement. The county sheriff was an elected official headquartered in the county seat, not Stone Harbor. The officer I had visited with in Stone Harbor was appointed by the sheriff as a deputy sheriff.

The island home of the hostile lobstermen was actually in another county and local law enforcement was provided by another deputy sheriff. Apparently these two men were attempting to work together to prevent violence between the two groups of lobstermen.

I couldn't prove anything and needed to learn more as I was now convinced Nancy's photos had placed her in serious danger. Why?

#   #   #

To date, gossip at lunch and eavesdropping in the afternoon had been my best sources of local information. I had learned at the cafe that Rob's old mate, Danny, had previously been given permission by Mary Alice to move Rob's boat back to its mooring after it had been "inspected and released" by the sheriff.

Sandy had said that Danny had told his friends that he was interested in buying the boat and wanted to start lobster fishing. It was unclear to me how this could happen since it was my understanding Danny had always been a sternman and did not yet have the required state license for lobster fishing.

Nancy had described the location to me where she had taken the missing photos and I had decided to investigate. The only camera I had owned was on my iPhone. I didn't see any reason to buy a camera I wouldn't know how to use so I had purchased a set of strong binoculars in Bangor before I returned to Stone Harbor.

#　　#　　#

I departed the Inn early Tuesday morning but didn't take my morning walk. Instead I got in my rental car and located Nancy's vantage point along the road to the art camp. I actually drove out to the art camp for the first time and backtracked to make certain I had the right location.

The location Nancy had selected was actually an informal observation point where there was space to park a couple of cars just off the road. A short path led from the parking area to a hiking trail and an overlook of the open ocean and a small cove.

Nancy had told me she had stopped along the road one morning on the way to the art camp and discovered what she considered to be a perfect location for early morning photos. Nancy told me she had noticed the area because both hikers and sightseers frequently parked their cars in that location.

Nancy was right - that location provided a great view of both the open ocean with hundreds of lobster buoys reflecting in the sunlight and of the cove where Rob's boat was moored.

Working Lobster Boat

I was fascinated by the activities of the lobstermen out on the ocean. They appeared to drive their boats in circles to find their buoys and pick up their lobster traps. With my new binoculars I could clearly observe the people working on the boats and I was pleased that I now had a better understanding about what they were doing.

I returned late that afternoon and saw mostly sailboats out for the day since the lobster boats work in the morning. When I turned my focus back to Rob's boat, I was surprised to see someone onboard who then returned by dinghy to a small floating dock. I didn't get a good look at the man as he got into a dark blue pickup truck and drove away. I assumed it was Rob's old mate Danny just checking on the boat.

I frankly had no idea what else to do and planned to continue my visits to Nancy's observation post each morning before breakfast and each evening before going to dinner.

I enjoyed observing the lobstermen work their traps in the morning and my visits in the evening promised to provide spectacular views of the sunset just as Nancy had predicted.

#   #   #

Anne approached me after breakfast at the Inn on Wednesday morning and asked;

"Would you be interested in joining Barbara and a couple of her students this morning for a short cruise on my boat? The schooners are sailing nearby today and we always enjoy photographing them under sail."

"Absolutely, that sounds like fun."

Anne drove us over to a small cove near town where the pleasure boats are kept on their moorings.

Anne explained; "Stone Harbor is a working lobster fishing town and the lobster boats have priority on the moorings in the town harbor."

We met Barbara and two of her students at the dinghy dock and Anne took a couple of trips to get us all out to her boat. I was impressed, both Anne and Barbara were very capable, the dinghy was tied to the mooring, the boat inspected and we were underway.

Duffy 37 on a Mooring

Anne was right. Her boat had a very nice teak wood interior with a settee and table in the main cabin. The boat had a full galley, enclosed head with a separate shower and a stateroom with lots of storage in the cabin space below.

Anne explained; "Maine has some amazing boat builders. Boat yards in places like Brooklin and Rockport build some very beautiful custom sailing yachts. Other smaller shops finish custom interiors like this on real lobster boats. Some people would call my Duffy 37 a lobster yacht."

"The only downside is Maine's short boating season, but it's really beautiful between late June and early October. I will need to put the boat back in the storage barn for the winter in a few weeks."

In less than an hour we had entered a time warp and were surrounded by several classic sailing schooners that took us back in time. Barbara's students were busy with their cameras!

Maine Schooners Under Sail

Anne explained; "People can book a cabin on one of these boats and enjoy a week cruise along the coast of Maine. That's why you see so many people on deck waving at us."

The five of us enjoyed a sandwich onboard that afternoon and I was now completely convinced that I needed to consider boating as part of my future retirement plan.

Anne drove us back to the Inn and as we parted I said;

"Anne, that was a wonderful day. I really can't thank you enough for inviting me to join you and Barbara. You have a fantastic boat and I can certainly see why you enjoy it."

#   #   #

Wednesday evening the weather had turned somewhat rainy and had become very foggy. I didn't expect much of a sunset and wanted to make it a short visit to the observation point and head back to the Inn. I decided to stay longer when I again saw activity on Rob's boat.

That evening the man I thought was Danny released the boat from its mooring and moved it to a small floating dock. A black pickup truck then parked next to Danny's dark blue pickup and the driver unloaded two bait totes that were wrapped with the same type of tape I had seen on the totes in Nancy's photos. The bait totes were carried to Rob's boat by both men.

Once aboard, the two men spoke briefly and then

the driver of the black truck departed. The fog was growing thicker but I was convinced the driver of that black truck was the same tall and slender man that had been in Nancy's photo with Rob. I had nicknamed him Red as he clearly had red hair. To my surprise Danny did not return Rob's boat to its mooring but instead headed out to sea in the fog.

I doubted Danny was going fishing as he didn't have his lobster fishing license and all of Rob's lobster traps had been pulled and stacked at his old house pending settlement of his estate. No lobster fishing gear was on the boat. What was Danny doing?

#   #   #

When I returned to my room I opened the iPad and again looked at Nancy's photos. The black pickup that had arrived that evening certainly looked to be the same as the one in the photo the night before Rob died. I was now even more certain that its driver was the man I now called Red.

All my suspicions were still circumstantial but I was convinced I was beginning to see the pieces of the puzzle that I needed to arrange to solve the mystery of Nancy's missing photos.

It appeared that Rob's old sternman Danny had now been recruited by Red to do something with the same bait totes that had been loaded on Rob's boat in Nancy's photos. So, who was Red, what was in those bait totes and what were they doing with them?

My early morning drive the next day confirmed that Rob's boat was back on its mooring with no bait totes on deck.

12

On Thursday morning at breakfast I had my usual brief friendly morning visit with Anne. Our topic was mostly about the weather as the rain had now intensified so I had only taken a short time for my early morning drive and after breakfast I passed on taking coffee to the Fisherman's deck. I was surprised when Anne asked:

"Did the rain stop you from going for your early morning drive?"

"No, but it will prevent my morning walk and working on the Fisherman's deck today. Guess I will just work in my room."

Having a rainy morning to work in my room was probably a good thing. I have always started any written analysis in my small notebook to help organize my thoughts and then try to finalize my thoughts in a more organized fashion on my laptop.

My notebook was now separated into two sections,

notes for my book and notes for the events related to Nancy's photos. The section for my book showed some progress that would some day help me finish my mystery novel. Unfortunately, I had not recently added much to the section for my book as I had become completely distracted by the mystery related to Nancy's missing photos.

The section in my notebook for Nancy contained a growing outline of all my observations and suspicions. During my audit career my approach was always to arrange all the pieces of a financial puzzle in such a way that I could consider multiple alternatives. It was always difficult to keep an open mind but preconceived ideas were seldom the right answer.

As a bank auditor, I had access to a wide range of resources to help solve a financial mystery. Seldom had I felt any personal risk as nearly all of my work was done inside an office on a computer at a desk. I had traveled to many of the bank's foreign offices to conduct investigations but again my work was inside the bank's offices at a computer, not doing field investigations.

I had received some personal threats related to several of my fraud and money laundering investigations at the bank and, as a result, I had moved to a very secure building near the United Nations in New York several years ago. It was a great location as I didn't need or own a car. I could walk to work for some exercise and the diplomates from foreign countries that also lived in the building made certain the entire building was secure and well protected.

However, I was now clearly out of my element and I was unable to unitize any of my previous resources. I was on my own and had growing concern for Nancy's safety and possibly my own if my interest in Nancy's photos would be discovered.

I did decide to venture out to lunch at the cafe that day. It was a nice break but all the conversation was about the nasty weather that was expected to last for several more days.

When I returned to the Inn I waited a few minutes to start work until Sally finished cleaning my bathroom. I had almost forgotten that Anne did have help at the Inn. Out of sight is frequently out of mind.

The rain continued that afternoon and I continued to think about the questions I had summarized on a page in my notebook:

> Nancy's missing photos? Why important?
> Who is the man with red hair? Red?
> Rob's death - accident or murder?
> If murder - by Red or Island Boat?
> Contents of bait totes?
> Nancy's contact information?

> How was her contact info obtained?
> Mary Alice's overdose - source of drugs?
> Danny's relationship to Red?

I had a growing list of questions and no answers.

The local deputy sheriff seemed to think the Medical Examiner's reports confirmed that both deaths were accidental and his actions seemed to indicate both these cases were closed. He appeared to be completely focused on preventing a potential lobster war.

My research had indicated that drugs were a major issue across all of New England so it was not a surprise that drugs could be an issue in Stone Harbor. However, other than gossip about Mary Alice's overdose I had overheard no other local speculation or conversation concerning drugs.

On my daily walks I had seen a number of black pickup trucks and the pickup appeared to be the primary mode of transportation for the local residents. I had not seen anybody that resembled Red on any of my walks around town and now assumed he was not local.

I had concluded the most important questions related to Nancy's missing photos were the identity of the man I called Red and the contents of those missing bait totes. I am not a detective and had no idea how to proceed. I had my suspicions but also knew from experience that it's foolish to jump to conclusions without solid evidence.

I knew I also needed to keep an open mind. I had no evidence that Red was actually involved in Rob's death and both men might have returned to Rob's dock that night. Rob could have met his death at the hand of a lobsterman from the island or it could just have been an accident.

But then, why did someone remove those photos and who had threatened Nancy? Why were those photos so important?

13

The rain continued that Thursday afternoon so I again skipped my afternoon beer on the Fisherman's deck. I decided to take my late afternoon break down in the Inn's living room.

I was greeted by Mr. & Mrs. Morrison, new guests that had arrived the first of the week. As usual, Anne had introduced us at at breakfast but all I recalled was that they were retired and visiting from Miami. They had a bottle of wine and offered me a glass.

They were very curious about lobster fishing and this became our topic of conversation on that late afternoon. I enjoyed telling them about my adventure on the lobster boat tour.

They had apparently overheard some conversation about Rob's tragic accident and asked if I had been at the Inn when his accident occurred. When I answered "yes" they asked if I heard any local gossip. I wanted to avoid this conversation but they were insistent and I was drinking their wine.

I limited my comments to the fact it seemed unusual that he had been working alone. I probably said too much when I commented it was sad his wife had died of a drug overdose the following week. This was apparently news to them and it started a whole new conversation about news reports they had read about drug issues in New England.

The Morrisons launched into all kinds of conspiracy theories about drug distribution and addiction in New England which I found somewhat surprising as they were from South Florida. I guess they thought coming from an area noted for drug trafficking made them experts. In any event, they were certain all local authorities were on the "take".

About this time I was aware that Anne had entered the room and was looking very uncomfortable overhearing the Morrisons' conspiracy theories about events in Stone Harbor.

Anne skillfully changed the subject back to the weather. I appreciated Anne's change of subject since I could now avoid any reaction to their theories.

The Morrisons said they were getting cabin fever and went back to their room to get some rain gear and headed over to the Fisherman's for dinner. I declined their invitation to join them for dinner as I did not want to get involved in another conversation with them in a public restaurant.

After they left the living room I asked Anne if it was possible to get some scrambled eggs or something else to eat so I could stay at the Inn.

"No problem, join me in the breakfast room in an hour."

#   #   #

I really didn't expect Anne to say "yes". I had seen no change in her normal friendly but professional manner after our lobster boat voyage with Barbara. That boat trip was not mentioned again after we returned to the Inn.

I had no reason to go back to my room so I just stayed in the living room and read a magazine article about travel in Maine and looked at the L.L.Bean catalog to occupy my time. I then walked over to the breakfast room to meet Anne as she had requested.

Anne was not in the breakfast room when I arrived but she walked in from the kitchen door a few minutes later. Anne said "please join me" and motioned me through the kitchen door down a short hallway and into another cozy living room with a small table set for two.

"I don't want any of the guests to see anyone

eating dinner at the Inn so I hope you find this comfortable."

I certainly had noticed that Anne was an attractive brunette during my stay at the Inn but was surprised to see she had her hair down and had changed into what appeared to be a somewhat revealing dress with a stylish jacket. This was a complete change from her modest appearance over the past few weeks.

Her living quarters appeared more spacious than I had anticipated. She shared the kitchen with the Inn but had a nice living room with a cozy seating area with a small couch and two comfortable chairs facing a fireplace and the dining area where I was seated.

The living room also had several bookcases and a flat panel television. Several doors led off the main room and I could see a bedroom through a door that was slightly open. Anne had a very comfortable living area and I could see how she could disappear each evening.

Anne had prepared an omelet for the two of us and had offered me a glass of wine. We then enjoyed a mushroom omelet, a glass of chardonnay and some friendly conversation together.

"I must admit, I was relieved when Nancy responded to my messages and reported she left because of a family emergency."

I responded; "Frankly, so was I. She looked really upset when I saw her depart the Fisherman's deck that morning."

Anne said; "It was nice when she was recognized by her workshop but really strange that some of those great photos went missing. What do think that was about?"

"I haven't a clue; it's a mystery why anybody would take them unless they thought they would make a great souvenir. Still they should have asked permission."

Even though I had grown to like Anne I still didn't want to share what I had learned about Nancy's missing photos or any of my suspicions.

As we ate, our conversation and Anne's questions became more personal.

"Steve, how did you get into the accounting profession?"

"I was raised in a small town in Kentucky and started my banking career as a part-time teller at a small community bank in Kentucky while attending college. The bank offered me a job as a junior auditor following my graduation with an accounting degree."

"So how did you get from that small bank in Kentucky to your position with the bank in New York?"

"Well, as you probably know, larger banks have been buying smaller banks across the country. My audit career followed a series of bank acquisitions that took me to Louisville, Chicago and finally about fifteen years ago to the bank's headquarters in New York City. My retirement account indicates I worked thirty-five years without ever changing my employer, just the name of the bank on my paycheck."

Anne then asked; "How are you adjusting to retirement?"

I responded; "Anne, I had always been completely focused on my job and had not really given much thought to my retirement. Frankly, I am just starting to think about ways to occupy my time."

"The first month of this trip seemed more like a vacation than retirement. However, my previous vacations were always interrupted by 'emergency' calls from the office but my cell phone is now silent."

"Steve, when you arrived you said you were planning to write a murder mystery. How is your book coming along?"

"Slow, I must admit I sometimes get writer's block but I am making good progress. It all started when some friends suggested I write a book about the interesting cases I helped solve."

"My length of service with the bank gave me the option of taking early retirement this year and I was ready to start a new chapter in my life. My story is based on a recent money laundering case involving cryptocurrency. Right now completing that book is my retirement plan."

Anne then responded; "My husband was a partner at one of the national accounting firms and we moved to Maine when he retired fifteen years ago. He didn't adjust well to retirement and quickly got bored. We sold our house in a nearby town and purchased the lobster boat for fun and this Inn as our retirement plan."

I added; "You have done a great job with the Inn. It's very comfortable and your decor certainly looks traditional Maine."

"It should, when we purchased the Inn it needed some work and new furniture. We decided to decorate with furnishings from L.L.Bean to provide a traditional Maine atmosphere."

"My husband died from a heart attack about seven years ago. I decided to keep the Inn as it keeps me busy and I enjoy meeting new people. I have good help so it's worked out but I must admit the winters seem longer every year."

"Steve, were you ever married?"

"Yes, but we got divorced when my job took me to Chicago and my wife didn't want to leave her family in Louisville. My job had become all consuming and it remained that way until my retirement early this summer."

"Do you have any children?"

"No, we were both too busy at the time to start planning a family."

I asked in return; "Do you?"

"Ours was a second marriage for my husband. I was working before we got married and we did not have children either."

We had finished eating and Anne suggested we move to a more comfortable seating area. She cleared the table and excused herself for a minute. I had taken a seat on the couch and when Anne returned she sat across from me in one of the comfortable chairs.

Anne then resumed the conversation about my career. Since her husband had been an accountant she was well versed in asking about my job.

She then changed the subject back to my book.

"Was your lobster boat tour related to your book? You seem to have an interest in lobster fishing."

"No, I am just a curious person and learning new things during my travels has always been a habit."

Anne said: "It's really sad that both Rob and Mary Alice died recently; so glad they didn't have any children. Mary Alice was a nice girl, she actually worked at the Inn for a couple of years when she was in high school."

I ventured to ask: "Did you ever suspect she had a drug habit?"

"No, but both Mary Alice and Rob kind of drifted away over the past couple of years. Guess that might have been when it started but I don't know."

Anne got up to top up our wine glasses and when she returned she had removed her jacket and joined me on the small couch. Anne was certainly an attractive woman but I was growing uncomfortable with both her changing appearance and her personal questions.

I just didn't know if I could trust Anne and I did not want to discuss my suspicions about Nancy's photos nor about Rob's or Mary Alice's deaths.

I tried to change the subject; "You have nice living quarters. Do you stay in Maine all winter?"

"Yes, I have been but I think I will join some friends that have invited me to visit them in Florida this winter. What do you plan to do after you go back to New York?"

I responded; "I really have no plans but I also have friends that have invited me to Florida and it sounds like a good location when it gets cold."

We then had a very awkward silence sitting together on her small couch with our glasses of wine.

I finally broke the silence; "Well, I thank you for a very nice omelet but it's probably time for me to go."

I was very confused and conflicted about my feelings for Anne as I walked back to my room.

14

Friday morning was clear and sunny and my view of the lobster boats working offshore was fantastic. On the other hand, Rob's boat remained at its mooring with no activity. When I returned to my rental car I noticed the rental car agreement was on the floor rather than in the door side pocket where I kept it. I kept nothing of value in the car so had no reason to always keep it locked. Was I now becoming paranoid or had someone actually searched my car?

Anne greeted me with her usual warm but professional welcome at breakfast that morning. She acted as if nothing had occurred the night before and I hoped I didn't show how uneasy I felt. My relationship with Anne felt more awkward to me after our evening dinner together.

Lunch at the cafe took an unexpected turn when the Morrisons joined me at the counter and resumed talking about their drug conspiracy theories related to Rob's and Mary Alice's deaths.

Their intrusion and conversation was not welcomed by me nor the local crowd. News of that unwelcome lunch conversation traveled fast and I could sense a more reserved greeting when Kathy served me my beer on the deck that afternoon.

"Good afternoon, are your friends going to join you?"

"What friends?"

"Heard you and your friends had some interesting theories about drug trafficking at lunch today."

"Kathy, those people are not my friends. They are guests at the Inn and just sat down next to me. They talk too loudly and I don't agree with their opinions."

"OK, but Sandy said some folks were mighty upset about the conversation."

The Morrisons had clearly bought some unwanted attention to me and I was suddenly feeling a little more like an outsider.

#   #   #

On Saturday morning I again drove out to the observation post and was watching the lobster boats with my binoculars when I was surprised with a greeting:

"How are you this morning?"

When I turned around I was approached by two teenage girls out for a morning hike.

I responded; "Just fine, it's a beautiful morning."

I am not much of an outdoor person and had not paid much attention to the hiking path that started near my parked car. The two teenagers started down the path. I decided nothing was happening with Rob's boat so I returned to the Inn for breakfast.

Thankfully the Morrisons had checked out that morning. When I returned to my room after breakfast, I noticed the door to the Morrison's room was open and Sally was just leaving after cleaning their room and changing the bed.

I had been preoccupied earlier that morning and now realized Sally had been one of the girls I had seen hiking. I always associated Sally with her colorful t-shirts advertising rock bands. Sally had been wearing a jacket and backpack for her hike that had covered up her signature trademark.

I said; "Hi, how was your hike?"

She smiled and said; "Great. You were right, it's a beautiful morning."

I then picked up my notebook and laptop from the desk in my room and walked over to the Fisherman's deck as usual. Shortly after I arrived I received a call on my cell phone from a number I didn't recognize. Like many folks I frequently received unwanted solicitations for vacations, credit cards and other so-called services and no longer answered every call to my cell phone.

A few minutes later I heard the ping that indicated a new message. I always checked my messages and was prepared to promptly delete it, assuming it was an unwanted solicitation.

To my surprise a male voice said;

"Mr Wilson, your interest in lobster fishing is a dangerous pursuit. You should return to New York."

#   #   #

That call confirmed that my identity and activities had been discovered. Just like Nancy, the caller had both my name and my cell phone number.

I thought I must be on the right path but just didn't know what was at the end of that path. I was completely convinced that Nancy's photos were the key to the mystery.

If I assumed drugs had some relationship to the deaths of both Rob and his wife then I needed to make the connection. According to the local lobstermen the DEA had not discovered drugs on Rob's boat. If drugs were not coming in on Rob's lobster boat then something related to drug trafficking might be going out.

Drug trafficking is a two-way activity - drugs into the country and money out of the country. Tracking money going out through the banking system had been my specialty. Drug dealers collect a lot of cash and people like me had made it increasingly difficult to pass it through the banking system. Was it possible that someone was now simply shipping cash out on Rob's boat?

If those bait totes were being used to transfer cash then I quickly estimated one bait tote could hold several million dollars in $100 dollar bills. Nancy's photos showed that two extra bait totes were taped shut and loaded on Rob's boat that night. If that was a standard shipment and Rob made one night trip each week then I calculated Rob could easily have moved over $100 million in cash offshore over the past year.

I had no idea if transferring cash offshore by boat was really feasible and where or how those bait totes could be transferred offshore. But the totes loaded on Rob's boat that night were no longer on his boat when it was towed back to the town dock. If my suspicions were correct that Red was involved in drug trafficking and associated with

Rob's death then it could certainly provide an incentive to destroy Nancy's photos.

But now someone, probably Red, suspected me of snooping and the Morrisons had created unwanted attention. I don't pretend to be a hero and decided it was time to act like I was taking my caller's advice seriously and depart town.

15

3rd Week of September

On Sunday morning after breakfast I told Anne that I would be checking out and planned to return home to New York on Monday. I told her I understood it was short notice and didn't expect a refund for the week. I was completely taken aback when Anne replied:

"I hope our dinner the other night hasn't contributed to your decision to leave early."

"Certainly not, I enjoyed our dinner very much."

#   #   #

Sunday evening I had booked my flight to Charlotte and arranged to rent a car. I said goodbye to Anne and drove to Bangor after breakfast on Monday and took my flight.

Whoever was making the phone calls had now obtained contact information for both Nancy and myself. The more I thought about it, the more I thought the source of our contact information had to be the registration cards at the Inn. This was the only common location that I could identify that had contact information for both of us.

I had grown increasingly uncomfortable with Anne's questions about my activities. It could be just an honest interest and paranoia on my part. At no time had I revealed any of my suspicions to Anne about why Nancy's photos had gone missing. I really didn't want to believe it but it certainly looked like the Inn could be the source of our contact information being obtained and somehow Anne might be involved.

#   #   #

I picked up my rental car in Charlotte and called Nancy to confirm that I was returning to the nearby motel that night. When I arrived, Nancy had also booked a room for herself and was waiting for me.

"Nancy, the bad news is that I received a warning call yesterday morning. It looks like someone has made the connection."

"I went to your observation post both morning and night last week. One night I witnessed the man I now call Red bring a taped bait tote just like the ones in your photos to Rob's old boat. Danny, Rob's old mate, then took the boat out to sea."

I brought her up to date on my activities and we decided to go to a nearby cafe for dinner. We did not have a plan and decided to stay another day and I told Nancy I planned to contact my friend Mark again the next day to ask his advice.

#   #   #

After dinner Monday night I was in my room sitting at a small desk that had a view of the front parking lot. My rental car was parked near a light in the parking lot and I observed a car pull into the lot and park near mine. I was shocked when I saw a man with what appeared to be red hair get out of his car and walk down the row toward my rental car. He then turned back to his car and drove away.

Was I being paranoid? Was that Red? How did he find me and identify my rental car? Was it possible that Red was tracking me to find Nancy - if so, we were both in trouble!

Nancy was in her room and I walked down the interior hallway and knocked on her door. We sat with a view of the front parking lot and I told her what I had witnessed.

Nancy became really frightened and I didn't want to admit how frightened I had become. We really had no long-term plan but we both thought it best to leave the motel that night and drive to Charlotte.

Nancy's car was parked in the back parking lot and we assumed we could risk departing unobserved by the back exit.

We both gathered our travel bags and took the back stairs down to the back parking lot. We observed no activity as we quickly walked to Nancy's car and she asked me to drive.

We started driving the twenty miles or so back toward the Interstate and to Charlotte. The drive would give us time to discuss a plan.

Shortly after we departed the motel I noticed lights in the rear view mirror but I was relieved when the car apparently pulled off and I didn't see anyone behind us.

A short while later I noticed headlights rapidly gaining on Nancy's car and then pull over to pass. I glanced over just as a large, dark blue SUV pulled along side.

"Shit!", I thought I recognized Red just as this large SUV slammed into us.

Nancy's car was forced off the highway and down a very steep embankment. Our airbags deployed and we came to stop against a large tree just short of a cliff that could have ended our journey permanently. Broken glass, dust and I feared some smoke seemed to be everywhere.

"Nancy, are you OK?"

"I don't know, everything hurts."

I was slowly able to move and open my car door. Nancy seemed trapped by the deflated airbag and her seatbelt and her side of the car was smashed against the tree. Nancy was alive but I was not certain I could get her out of the car.

I looked back up to the road. Was Red still around? Any doubt about his intentions were now erased - he intended to eliminate us both in another accident.

Fortunately, I didn't see anyone up on the road but there was not much moonlight so it was pretty dark. I located my cell phone in my pocket and tried to call 911 but I had no cell signal.

I then went around the car to Nancy's door. She was more composed at this point and said she had unfastened her seat belt and could move if I could open her door. We both suffered some minor cuts from the broken glass but neither of us appeared to have a serious injuries. I was able to open her door and she slowly climbed out of the car and sat on the grass leaning against a nearby tree.

Her car was badly damaged but we were both alive. Nancy was right, everything hurt but we were both able to walk. I was in better condition than Nancy and told her I would try to get back up to the road to get a cell signal so emergency response could locate us. It was a painful climb but I was able to reach the road. I was relieved when the SUV and Red were not in sight.

I had a cell signal up on the road and called 911.

"We just had a hit and run accident on Wilderness Highway just a few miles north of the Interstate. I think the woman with me might be badly injured."

"The car is located down the mountain and I am not sure if you can see it from the road. I will remain by the roadside to flag down help when it arrives."

Emergency response crew arrived quickly and we were soon joined by a highway patrol car, a tow truck and an ambulance. We assumed Red had traveled on as the highway patrolman had seen no damaged, dark blue SUV along the highway.

Over her objections, the ambulance crew placed Nancy on a stretcher to bring her back up to the road.

We were both taken to a nearby community hospital and were required to spend the night in their emergency room for observation to make certain we had not received any serious injuries or had suffered a concussion.

We were both released from the hospital Tuesday morning. Thankfully the airbags had done their job and our injuries were mostly superficial. We were both badly bruised with a lot of little cuts from the broken glass but we had no serious injuries.

Nancy's car was a total wreck and after release from the hospital emergency room I convinced Nancy it was time to return to familiar territory.

#   #   #

Late Tuesday morning Nancy called Jane out at the art colony and she gave us a ride from the hospital back to the motel so we could pick up my rental car.

I had convinced Nancy that my two-bedroom high-rise co-op apartment building had excellent security and was the safest location for both us. My contacts in government are mostly located in New York and it was now time for some personal visits to seek help.

Our drive during the day to Charlotte and flight to New York that night were both uneventful. When we arrived in New York I introduced Nancy to my building's doorman and he described the building's security systems to reassure her this was a safe location.

#   #   #

The highway patrol had issued a hit-and-run bulletin to law enforcement in North Carolina that indicated a dark blue SUV was suspected of forcing our car off the road. I was disappointed they would not identify Red as the possible driver. Nancy had cropped and enlarged a photo to show Red's face but they would not add the photo to the bulletin based on what they considered my uncertain identification.

I obtained a digital copy of the bulletin and sent it by email to the deputy sheriff in Stone Harbor. I then called the deputy on Wednesday:

"Sheriff, Nancy Olson, the photographer, and myself were just forced off the highway by an SUV and almost killed. I believe that SUV was driven by the second man in the photos that Nancy took of Rob's boat. Have you been able to locate and identify this man?"

"No, but I will let the Carolina folks know if I do."

That was it, no more conversation and the deputy sheriff ended the call.

The local deputy's lack of interest was very frustrating and continued to concern me. He appeared to have little or no interest in Red's identification or concern about our situation.

#   #   #

135

My list of unanswered questions was growing - not shrinking.

How did Red identify Nancy's car?

Red might have seen her parked car along the road the days Nancy was taking photos. He might know how to go online and find her home address and her tag number from public records. Finally, her car tag number was on the registration card at the Inn. Once again, it was certainly possible that the Inn was Red's source for Nancy's contact information. If so, how and why?

#   #   #

On Friday the highway patrol notified us they had located the hit-and-run car and driver. It was a local teenager with red hair that had been at a party and was under the influence when he hit our car. He admitted he was frightened and just kept driving. He was driving his parents SUV and told them he hit a deer on the way home. His father took the car to a repair shop the following day and the owner of the shop reported the suspicious damage to the highway patrol.

When the highway patrol examined the SUV they found paint that matched Nancy's car along the damaged side of the car. The local teenager confessed almost immediately after a highway patrol officer arrived at the teenager's home.

Nancy and I decided to contact a lawyer to explore damage and liability claims. However, we both told the lawyer our primary interest was making certain all medical expenses were paid by the family's insurance and a replacement for Nancy's car was arranged.

#   #   #

I had made a very big deal of the man I called Red as the driver in my conversations with both the highway patrol officers and the deputy sheriff and I was wrong. I was embarrassed and my credibility with the local deputy sheriff would be badly damaged. In some respects it was a relief that Red was not the guilty party and that it was just an unintended accident.

16

4th Week of September

I had arranged for Nancy and me to have dinner with Mark, my friend with the FBI, on Sunday night. I had previously discussed my suspicions about Red's connection to Nancy's missing photos with Mark. I trusted Mark's judgment and wanted to take this opportunity for Nancy to share her story with Mark in person.

Mark proceeded to summarize his understanding of the situation after listening very carefully to the two of us and asking a few questions;

"Nancy, let's make an effort to review the facts as we know them without confusing the issue with unsupported suspicions."

"First, your photos of Rob's lobster boat were removed from the library exhibit by persons unknown."

"The calls you have received from an unknown male have all been focused on obtaining the originals of the photos that were removed from the library."

"You have told me these photos are digital, not film, therefore it seems curious that this unknown person seems to think he can prevent distribution if he obtains the originals."

"My suggestion to you is to respond to his next text or email and say; "All of these photos are digital and they have been shared with law enforcement"."

"Nancy, if my assumption is correct, once this unknown male knows he cannot prevent future distribution then he will stop contacting you. We don't know why he wants your photos but he certainly doesn't want to attract the attention of law enforcement. He will need to stop contacting you and disappear."

"Thank you for saving and sharing some of your recent voice mails, text messages and emails with me. You should keep these. However, it's easy to buy a pre-paid throw away phone and to set up a fake email address. I suspect there is no way to trace these."

"Steve, we have known one another for many years and worked on many cases together. You certainly have a talent for solving financial crimes and I have grown to respect your suspicions."

"But for the moment, let's just deal with the facts we can confirm."

"First, your warning call referenced lobster fishing, not Nancy's photos. That doesn't mean they are not connected but it could be unrelated."

"Your suspicions of Red are based on his delivery of the two bait totes to Rob's boat that are visible in Nancy's photos and his subsequent delivery of similar bait totes to Rob's boat that you observed. We don't know what's in those bait totes and it could be nothing illegal."

"Nancy's photos do show that Red departed with Rob the night before Rob had his accident. However, they both could have returned to the dock that night and Rob then departed alone the next morning. Red may have no connection to Rob's death."

"You jumped to conclusions when you thought Red had been the driver that forced Nancy's car off the highway."

"Finally, the fact that Rob's wife died of an overdose does not indicate Rob was engaged in drug trafficking as he had no drugs on his boat nor were any found in his autopsy."

"I agree, these connections look suspicious but you have no evidence that either Red or Rob were engaged in anything illegal or that Red had anything to do with Rob's death."

"I suggest Nancy respond next time she receives a threat and you two sit tight for about a week and see if the messages to her stop."

#   #   #

My week with Nancy in New York was very pleasant but occasionally stressful. Nancy and I both jumped every time either of us got a call, text or email that week.

But Mark was right, Nancy received no additional calls, texts or emails after she replied to an email and indicated that the three photos had been shared with law enforcement. All contact with Nancy simply stopped.

I had received no new warning calls after my departure from Stone Harbor.

As the week progressed we got to know one another and enjoyed sharing time together. However, Nancy slept in the guest room and on Saturday, after the week in New York, Nancy decided it was time to end her "family emergency" and return to her job at the college.

17

1st week of October

I faced a dilemma and decided to discuss my thoughts over dinner with my friend Mark on Sunday night. Over time we had become both professional and personal friends.

Mark looks the role of a senior FBI agent - tall, dark hair and in good physical condition. He works out of the FBI's New York office and deals with financial cases nationwide. During my banking career we had spent untold hours working on cases together in his office. Our occasional dinners together were mostly business and I had never met his wife.

Over time I had learned that he is married with kids in college. He and his wife live on the upper west side of the city and she works in an art gallery. Mark has a diversity of personal interests and can comfortably discuss a wide range of topics.

I trust Mark's judgement and I was very pleased that he was willing to meet Nancy and discuss the events in Stone Harbor with me. I wanted his advice and asked his opinion at dinner.

"Mark, I still have many unanswered questions - do I just let it go?"

"Steve, it appears your friend Nancy is safe and all efforts to obtain her original photos have now stopped. You have received no additional warnings so it seems you are no longer of interest."

"So, why do you want to stay involved?"

"Mark, you have known me a long time and we worked on a lot of cases together. You know that once I started on a case I just didn't stop until it was solved. I just want to know what this is all about."

"Steve, my advice is for you to stay in New York and let the local authorities solve the mystery."

"Mark, I have no confidence that the deputy sheriff will even try to solve this mystery if I don't return to Stone Harbor."

#   #   #

Monday morning I called Anne: "I would like to return to the Inn if you have a room available. I find it the best place to work on my book."

Anne responded; "I can arrange a room. You are certainly welcome."

So on Tuesday I once again rented a car and drove to Stone Harbor. It was now the first week of October and the temperature was dropping. Most visitors to Maine were "Leaf Peepers" there to view the amazing colors of the leaves.

I stopped at L.L.Bean in Freeport on my way to Stone Harbor to purchase a more appropriate wardrobe for the colder weather. I was beginning to understand the joke about Maine having two seasons; winter and the 4th of July! Warm weather along the coast of Maine is really limited to July thru September.

On Wednesday afternoon, the day after my arrival, I received another warning call!

"Don't be stupid. Go back to New York."

This second warning call just confirmed my suspicions that I was on the right track. Before leaving New York I had arranged another personal meeting with the local deputy sheriff on Thursday morning. However, he was not happy to see me.

"Sheriff, first I received another warning call yesterday and I want you to listen to the phone message."

The deputy listened to the message and handed my iPhone back to me.

"Mr. Wilson, we don't know if that call has any relationship to Miss Olson's missing photos or Rob's death. I thought you understood that you had no business trying to investigate Rob's death. I have no obligation to report our findings to you but want you to know I did follow up on those photos taken the night before Rob's boat was found drifting."

"I checked back with some of Rob's neighbors about the possibility that Rob had taken his boat out the night before his death."

"One of Rob's neighbors told me that Rob had called him from his dock just before midnight the night before Rob's boat was found empty. Rob had apologized for the call but his truck had a dead battery and Mary Alice wasn't answering their phone. Rob wanted a jump to start his truck so he could drive home."

"So, Mr. Wilson, Rob did return to his dock and was still alive that night. We have no reason to question that Rob went out fishing alone the next morning and that his death was an accident."

"Now, my primary concern today is preventing conflict between Stone Harbor's lobstermen and the lobstermen from the island. We don't want another lobster war."

I asked; "Sheriff, have you asked Danny about the man who delivered those bait totes?"

The response was abrupt; "That's none of your business."

"Sheriff, both Miss Olson and I have received threatening calls. I believe the Inn is the most likely source of the contact information that our mysterious caller has used to make those calls. Can I at least ask you to show that red headed man's picture to the folks over at the Inn to see if anybody recognizes him?"

The deputy sheriff responded; "Mr. Wilson, if I agree to do that and nobody recognizes this man will you then agree to go back home to New York?"

It didn't look like I had much of a choice as I obviously wasn't very welcome any longer in Stone Harbor. I responded; "Yes."

#   #   #

That Friday afternoon the deputy called to tell me to meet him at the Inn. Anne was expecting him when he arrived.

"Anne, Mr. Wilson has located Miss Olson and she has provided me with a statement indicating the reason she left Stone Harbor was because she had received a disturbing phone call concerning those three photos that disappeared from the library."

"Mr. Wilson has discovered that Miss Olson's photos were taken of Rob's lobster boat the night before he died. Rob was with a man that night that we cannot identify."

The deputy handed Nancy's enlarged photo of Red to Anne; "Do you recognize this man?"

Anne looked puzzled and replied; "No, sorry he doesn't look familiar."

Anne then turned to me; "Steve, why didn't you mention you located Nancy? What's this about?"

I responded; "I don't know what this is about. I have also received several threatening messages and, other than the deputy, I didn't know who to get involved."

I then asked Anne; "Is it OK if the deputy shows this photo to your cook and Sally?"

Anne replied; "Certainly, Sam, the cook, has gone for the day but I think Sally is still upstairs cleaning. I will go get her."

Sally was a little nervous when she entered the room and saw the deputy sheriff in his uniform but relaxed when he smiled and offered her a friendly greeting. He then handed her the picture of Red.

Sally turned very pale with a shocked expression.

"Sally, do you recognize this man?"

"Why, what did he do?"

"Sally, how do you know this man?"

"Will I get in trouble?"

"Sally, I don't know of any trouble. I just want to know how you know this man."

"I don't know if I should tell you but I don't want to get in any trouble."

"Sally, you won't get in any trouble if you just tell us the truth about how you know this man."

"OK, I met him one night when I was visiting with Roxy, my sister, in Portland. She calls him Red and I think he might be her sometimes boyfriend."

"OK, thank you. How many times have you seen him?"

"Just twice, he doesn't hang around when I visit Roxy."

"Do you know where he lives or works?"

"No, Roxy just said he travels and makes a lot of

money so they can have a good time when he is in town."

"Sally, if I recall correctly, Sandy, down at the cafe, Mary Alice and Roxy all were friends in school. Is that right?"

"Yes, Roxy and Mary Alice were best friends. Roxy was really upset when Mary Alice died."

The deputy surprised me when he then asked; "Sally, does a good time involve drugs?"

Once again, Sally tuned pale and answered; "I don't want to get my sister in trouble."

"OK, no problem. How often do you and Roxy talk?"

"Almost every day."

"Does Roxy ever ask you to do her a favor?"

Sally again was getting very nervous and answered; "Sometimes."

"Has Roxy ever asked you about some of the guests at the Inn?"

Sally looked at Anne and asked; "Do I have to answer?"

The deputy responded; "Sally, it's best for you if you are truthful today."

"Anne, I am really sorry. Roxy just asked me to take a photo of Miss Olson's registration card. I had told Roxy that Miss Olson had some great photos on display at the library. Roxy said she was interested in learning more about photography and just wanted to know how to contact her."

The deputy then asked; "Roxy ever ask you about Mr. Wilson?"

"Sometimes, several weeks ago I just mentioned he seemed to be interested in Miss Olson's missing photos."

"What did Roxy say?"

Sally looked over at Anne and responded; "She asked me to take a photo of his registration card."

"Did you?"

"Yes. Roxy's my sister, I had to."

"Anything else?"

"I told Roxy that Mr. Wilson was back at the Inn this week and I happened to mention that he kept a notebook."

"What else?"

"Roxy asked me to take some pictures of the pages in Mr. Wilson's notebook."

"And, did you?"

"No, I said that was asking too much."

"OK, thank you. If you want to stay out of trouble you will not talk with Roxy about our conversation. Do you have her address in Portland?"

"Yes, but she's not there. Came home this morning. She told me Red got really angry and hit her so she had to come back home for a while."

"OK. If it's OK with Anne you can go back to work and remember it's best if you don't tell Roxy about our conversation."

Anne responded; "Sally, you know what you did was wrong. Thank you for being honest today. Go finish your work. We can talk about this later."

#   #   #

After Sally departed the deputy said; "Mr. Wilson, it looks like some of your suspicions might have merit. This is not my type of work and our county sheriff's office has a couple of people on staff that do investigations. I will tell them about this conversation and you should stick around until someone contacts you in the next few days."

With that the deputy sheriff drove off and Anne and I sat in an awkward silence for a while. Finally Anne said; "So, what's going on?"

"Anne, I really don't know where to start but I owe you an apology."

"I can explain in more detail if you want but I discovered that Nancy's missing photos were not taken in the morning. Those photos were taken of Rob's boat the night before he died."

"This man we call Red was with Rob on his boat that night and I suspected he had something to do with Rob's death."

"I saw the expression on Nancy's face the morning she got that phone call and drove off in such a hurry and then just seemed to disappear. I assumed Red made that call and he didn't want those photos in circulation for some reason and he threatened Nancy."

"My job at the bank involved doing investigations and by doing some research I was able to locate Nancy at an art colony in North Carolina. I talked with her at the art colony and she confirmed she was being threatened. I was convinced those threats were from Red."

"It's a long story, but Nancy and I were in her car when it was forced off the road and down a mountainside in North Carolina. I was convinced that Red was the driver of the car that slammed into us."

"I was wrong, we were forced off the road by a drunk teenager with red hair. I lost a lot of credibility with the deputy with my false accusation."

"In addition, the deputy just told me that one of Rob's neighbors had confirmed that Rob returned to his house that night so the deputy doesn't think Red was involved in Rob's death."

"I don't know why Nancy and I are being threatened but it has something to do with her photos. I believed that the most likely source of the personal information used by our caller to threaten us was from the registration cards here at the Inn. Yesterday I finally convinced the deputy to at least come over and ask if anybody recognized Red."

"I want you to know that in return, the deputy asked me to leave town if nobody at the Inn recognized that man."

"Anne, if I was right that the registration cards were the source of Red's information then I really didn't know whom I could trust. I apologize."

Anne, just got up and walked out of the room.

# # #

Anne was her normal, professional self when she served breakfast to the guests the next morning. After breakfast, I told her I still planned to stay a while longer in Stone Harbor and asked if it was OK if I continued to stay at the Inn.

"Yes, it's OK, I need the business."

After the warning call I was concerned about going to the observation post to see if Red and Danny were still engaged in night trips. As a result, my only source of information that weekend was gossip at lunch and eavesdropping in the afternoon. Both Sandy and Kathy seemed to have forgiven me for having lunch with the Morrisons and were once again friendly and happy to have me as a returning customer.

On Saturday morning, the deputy called to tell me to expect a visit from an investigator early the next week.

18

2nd Week of October

I tried to focus on my novel while I waited for a call from the local investigator. Gossip at lunch and conversation at the Pub was increasingly focused on the conflict with the lobstermen from the nearby island.

As I suspected, Max and the other lobstermen were placing traps in the disputed area and arguments with the lobstermen from the island were occurring almost daily.

Apparently the deputy sheriffs from both areas were talking with the lobstermen and warning them not to start a war as violence would not be tolerated. Max and his friends were clearly frustrated with the situation.

I overheard some comments from Max on Monday afternoon that caught my attention.

"Had a great trip on our boat to Nova Scotia over the weekend with my wife and daughter to visit my wife's sister. The weather was perfect and it was great to get away from this shit for a few days."

"We came back last night and I'll be damned if we didn't see Rob's old boat. Hell if I know what it was doing out there in the middle of the night."

"Do you think Danny was out for some reason?"

Max replied; "Don't know, didn't stop to ask."

"Think that deputy is ever going to question those island folks about Rob's death?"

Max replied; "Maybe if we create enough heat out on the water those guys will start paying attention. Something's not right and neither deputy wants to play detective. Damn shame!"

The fact that Max had seen Rob's boat out in the middle of the night was encouraging to me, maybe I would get a break.

I was looking forward to meeting the investigator in a few days. I had heard nothing more from the deputy after our meeting at the Inn.

# # #

On Tuesday I received a call from an unknown local number and, as usual, did not want to answer. I did listen to the message when I heard the ping.

"Mr. Wilson? My name is Amanda Smith and I am an investigator with the county sheriff's office. I would like to stop by the Inn to visit with you this morning. Please return my call."

We arranged to meet at 11AM and I was surprised to see a tall, very attractive young woman with a blonde pony tail enter the Inn carrying a small backpack and wearing blue jeans and a bright red sweater. She approached me and said;

"Mr. Wilson, I am Amanda Smith. Please call me Amanda."

I responded "Yes, I'm Steve Wilson. Please call me Steve. The living room is currently empty if that's OK. We might need to move for more privacy if anybody decides to join us."

"Amanda, I expected someone in uniform."

"I find most people are much more comfortable and open with me if I am not in uniform. I want people to relax and talk to me."

Amanda was good at her job and we visited for about an hour while I answered her questions and described events to date. Her questions certainly indicated she was already well informed and I assumed the deputy had provided her with an extensive background briefing before her visit with me.

As she concluded her questions she asked; "Anything new you want to talk about?"

"Yes, Amanda, I just overheard Max say that he came across Rob's boat in the middle of the night on his return trip from Nova Scotia this past weekend. Why don't you talk to Max and maybe have a conversation with Danny about Red?"

I also asked; "Have you or the deputy talked with Roxy?"

"Yes, Roxy is frightened and not very helpful, yet."

19

I now recognized Amanda's number and answered when she called me the next day. We arranged to meet again at the Inn that afternoon.

"Steve, I think we need to talk. Your friend Mark at the FBI told me I could trust you and that you had helped them solve dozens of financial crimes before you retired."

I was somewhat intrigued by her comment, I didn't remember mentioning Mark to Amanda but decided to let it pass.

Amanda then said; "For your information, the deputy sheriff and I have talked with Danny on two occasions.

"The first time was a week ago when the deputy showed Danny the picture of Red. Danny told him he had no idea who that might be and had never seen the man."

"The second time was yesterday when I stopped by

to talk with Danny. I asked why Max had seen him out in the middle the night. Danny said Max must have been seeing things. He said neither he nor that boat had ever been out at night."

"I know I look young and I know some men don't take me seriously but I can tell when a man is lying to me and Danny was full of shit. I don't like being played for a fool. So, tell me, what do you think is going on?"

I replied; "For some reason the DEA searched Rob's boat on several occasions. Do you know why?"

"Feds don't tell me anything but I got word they suspected him of running drugs into the country."

"I am beginning to think they were right about a drug connection but were searching for the wrong thing. The answer is in those bait totes that Red was putting on that boat."

"Amanda, I still think this has something to do with drugs, something went wrong and Red has something to do with Rob's death. I just have no idea how to connect the dots."

#   #   #

Two days later Amanda came by the Inn to visit with me again.

"I had an interesting talk with Danny yesterday. When I mentioned he might be a possible accessory to the murder of Rob, it opened him right up."

"Said he had seen Red once talking to Rob right before Rob told him he was going to start working alone. Rob always was a stubborn independent guy so he wasn't too surprised when Rob told him he was not going to need him. Danny thought he must have made Rob mad or something and they would start working together again after he cooled down."

"Danny said Red looked him up when Rob showed up dead. Said Red knew he worked on Rob's boat and he had a business proposition that could help him make some money. Danny said he hadn't been working much and making some money sounded good."

"Danny said Red paid him to use Rob's boat just to make a delivery of a couple of bait totes to a fishing trawler offshore. He said Red would call him the day before making the delivery to make arrangements."

"Danny said he had used Rob's boat to go out at night and had made two deliveries so far. That's all he knows and he's got nothing to do with Rob's death."

"I told him to forget our conversation and to call

me the next time he heard from Red. Maybe we can intercept Red and find out what's in those bait totes."

"So, Steve, it looks like your suspicion about sending something offshore was right. Wonder what's in the totes and what went wrong?"

# # #

I was surprised when Sally appeared a short time after Amanda left the Inn.

"I saw you talking with that police woman."

"Yes."

"She talked to Roxy and Roxy's really frightened. I told Roxy how you helped Miss Olson and told Roxy she should talk to you."

"Sally, I am happy to talk with Roxy but don't know if I can help."

"That's OK, she needs to talk to someone and I don't know who else to suggest."

# # #

Sandy was full of gossip at lunch on Saturday.

"Rumor has it - that deputy been askin' around

again about Mary Alice and drugs being available in town. Her brother's still mighty upset about her overdose and blames Rob for gettin' her into heroin."

"Don't say I told you but Kathy said Roxy is back in town and she heard Roxy's really upset about Mary Alice's overdose. Anybody seen Roxy since she's been back?"

I was relieved that the gossip didn't include anything about Danny, Rob's boat or the deputy's conversation with Sally at the Inn. I grew up in a small town and never understood how some secrets became the topic for gossip and others remained a secret.

Maybe this deputy sheriff or Amanda had a clever way of spreading rumors to see what comes to the surface. I had to admit I had been impressed with the professional way that the young deputy had questioned Sally.

I called Amanda to tell her about Sally's visit. Sally had now arranged for Roxy to meet with me at the Inn on Sunday morning. I wanted to ask Amanda's advice and make certain she approved of my talking with Roxy.

Amanda replied; "Yes, go ahead, let's see if she will tell you anything that helps. She doesn't want to talk to me."

20

3rd Week of October

Roxy and Sally both showed up at the Inn as promised on Sunday morning. Roxy appeared to be in her mid-twenties and certainly resembled her teenage sister. Both were about five and half feet tall with blonde hair and blue eyes with an athletic appearance that indicated they both liked outdoor activities.

Once we were introduced, Roxy told Sally; "Get lost."

"Sally tells me you were able to help Miss Olson. That right?"

"Yes, she had been receiving threatening calls, texts and emails and we came up with a plan that stopped the threats."

"OK, I got to talk to somebody about getting help and I don't trust that deputy sheriff or that woman who talked to me."

I asked; "What's going on? Please talk to me about this man you call Red."

"I met Red at a bar after I moved to Portland a few years ago. He seemed real nice and we went out a couple of times."

"One night he asked if I wanted to try something that would make me feel amazing. I trusted the guy and said yes. It was something he called ecstasy I took that night. He was right and we had an amazing night together."

"I never took any other drugs and I hate needles. I only took ecstasy a few times when he visited. I didn't want to take it every time."

I asked; "Do you know where he gets the drugs or where he lives?"

"No, and we never went to his place but I don't think he lives in Portland."

I asked; "What else?"

"Well, one night he stopped by unannounced when Mary Alice was visiting. Mary Alice and I had been best friends since we were kids and she liked to visit me in Portland. We were both small town girls that enjoyed going out in a busy city."

"Rob and Mary Alice are both dead now so I guess

I can tell you what happened."

"Mary Alice got hurt about a year ago in a car accident. The doctors had her on some type of drug to help with her pain."

"The problem was Mary Alice got hooked on that drug and then the doctors stopped giving her the prescription. Red told her he could help and said he could arrange to get some type of opioid for her."

"Mary Alice told me a few days later that Red had arranged for a local dealer to deliver opioids to her for cash. She was worried about the cost as their insurance wouldn't pay for an illegal drug. I think that Red might also have offered to deliver it personally and trade sex for the opioids like I suspected he did with some other women."

"I found out later that Mary Alice really liked taking stuff and she got hooked on heroin. Mary Alice didn't have enough money to buy it and she couldn't get away very often to trade sex with Red to support her habit so somehow I think she got Rob and Red together."

"I don't know what their business arrangement was but I once overheard Red talking to someone on his phone about paying cash to Rob for doing some delivery. I guess that's how they got enough cash to pay the local dealer for her heroin."

"Red was with me one night when I got a call from Sally sometime in August. I said I can't talk right now Red's in town. Sally said that's interesting, I just saw his photo as part of the library's new exhibit."

"Red got really anxious when he heard that and he told me to have Sally get those photos and destroy them. He wanted to know who took them. Sally told me it was Miss Olson, a guest at the Inn. Red told me to have Sally get her contact information."

I asked; "Why did he want my personal contact information?"

"Sally had told me you seemed very interested in what happened to Miss Olson's photos and why she left town. When I mentioned that to Red he told me to have Sally get your contact information."

"He seemed to get nervous when I told him you were writing a murder mystery. Sally had already told me that you kept a notebook. He really wanted Sally to take some photos of your notebook for him after you returned to Stone Harbor."

"When Sally refused he got very angry and started hitting me. He never did that before and I got frightened and decided to come back home."

I asked; "Has Red tried to contact you?"

"Yea, he called a couple of times and told me that if I know what's good for me I won't talk about any of this with that deputy or police woman again."

I thanked Roxy for talking with me. I told her to go back home and that I would try to help.

After Roxy left I called Amanda and told her about my conversation with Roxy. Amanda said;

"Thanks, well done. That's all I need to know for now."

21

It was now mid-October but Monday afternoon was still just warm enough for me to sit on the deck above the Pub if I wore my new L.L.Bean coat. Later that afternoon I overheard more conversation about Mary Alice's brother. Like Rob, her brother was one of the younger lobstermen that didn't hang out much with the older group at the Fisherman's Pub. I had heard references to his anger in the past and it was again a topic of conversation.

"That boy just can't let it go. He blames Rob for his sister's death but Rob was already dead."

"Yea, he told me Rob got his sister started on heroin. That's why he blames him."

"Both Mary Alice and Rob are dead now; no point in carrying on so much. Can't do nothin' about it."

"Brother's anger nothin' new; saw him in a fight with Rob couple of weeks before Rob died."

\#   \#   \#

I was very embarrassed about suspecting that Anne was possibly involved in providing both Nancy's and my contact information to Red and had been trying to make amends. The Inn did not provide a really private time to talk unless Anne invited me to dinner in her living room and that was clearly not going to happen again.

However, I had persisted with invitations to have dinner in a nearby town and Anne had finally accepted for Tuesday night. I hoped this would give me an opportunity to make amends.

We had a candid conversation and a good meal but our relationship was far from warm and friendly. When we walked out to my rental car we found all four tires had been slashed!

While standing there in shock I got a call on my cell phone from an unknown number. As usual, I did not answer as I certainly didn't need to win a free trip that night.

Anne called a local towing service and she told them I needed four new tires installed. It certainly helps to have local knowledge and a truck with four new tires appeared in about thirty minutes.

I tried not to speculate about who was responsible and did not want to worry Anne. However, while waiting I did check my messages.

"Steve, you were warned not to stay in Stone Harbor."

I decided it was time for secrets to end and it would be best to let Anne listen to that message. That was the right decision because Anne's attitude changed to one of more understanding. To my surprise Anne said "Thank You" and reached for my hand.

We drove back to the Inn that night in silence but I could tell that Anne's displeasure with me was dissipating.

I called Amanda the next morning after breakfast and told her what happened and played the message for her. Amanda said; " I appreciate your help but it's OK with me if you want to leave town."

I responded; "Leaving town might be smart but I am too stubborn and plan to stay."

# # #

I was now more comfortable with Anne; however, I did not share any details with her about my meeting with Roxy or my conversations with Amanda.

The hot rumors at lunch Wednesday were about

Max's arguments with the lobstermen from the island and how the deputy sheriffs were working to keep the peace. Tensions were running high as the rumors openly speculated that one of the island's boats was involved in Rob's death. The local lobstermen were becoming even more convinced someone from the island was responsible for Rob's death and the island's lobstermen resented the accusation.

Max and his friends were not helping the situation since they were all placing traps in waters that were historically claimed by the island's lobstermen. In return, many of the island boats were now placing traps in waters claimed by the Stone Harbor lobstermen. The situation had escalated day-by-day with more frequent confrontations.

#   #   #

An announcement by the sheriff's office on Thursday hit both communities like a bomb going off in their harbors. The sheriff's office announced they had arrested Dave, Mary Alice's brother, and charged him with the death of his sister's husband, Rob.

If the sheriff's announcement was right, then I had been wrong again and Red was apparently not involved in Rob's death. I wanted to know more so took a chance and invited Amanda to dinner that night. She accepted on the condition we go to the same out-of-town restaurant where my tires had been slashed. Admittedly, I didn't want to order a new set of tires but my curiosity prevailed.

At dinner, Amanda told me she was only willing to share the facts that were in Dave's confession and would not share any additional information about their investigation.

"Dave admitted that he had started several fights with Rob as he thought Rob was the reason his sister was on heroin."

"Dave said he had encountered Rob that morning while pulling traps in the same area and Dave admitted he had started harassing Rob."

"Dave said at one point their boats were side-by-side and he took a swing with his boat hook in Rob's direction. Rob didn't duck in time and the boat hook hit Rob in the head and he fell to the deck."

"Dave thought Rob was just stunned but when Rob didn't get up he decided to go aboard Rob's boat and see what had happened. Dave said Rob wasn't breathing and had no pulse. He panicked and decided to fake the accident."

"Dave said fog had closed in during their encounter so nobody saw what happened. He just moved away and started pulling his traps in another area."

I told Amanda I appreciated her having dinner with me and sharing this information about Rob's death. Once again my suspicions about Red were wrong. Red was not the driver of the car that ran Nancy and me off the road and now, Red was not responsible for Rob's death.

I asked; "Does this mean the case is solved and you head back to your office?"

She replied; "No, you and Miss Olson have both received numerous threats that appear to be related to those missing photos. There is more to this story and I plan to solve that mystery."

Thankfully when we started our drive back to Stone Harbor my car still had four good tires. I was still paranoid about the tire slashing and told Amanda; "I think that car might be following us."

She replied; "Probably, the deputy is heading back with us. He staked out your car tonight in case your mystery person made an appearance. Dave didn't make those calls or slash your tires and we thought it was worth taking a chance that the person responsible might show up again."

I drove Amanda back to her car that was parked next to the deputy's office and she drove away. I had no idea where Amanda stayed in Stone Harbor.

#   #   #

The announcement that Dave had been responsible for Rob's death helped lower the tensions surrounding the potential lobster war. Both sides had been angry about the suspicion that Rob's death had been related to their fishing dispute.

I was impressed that my eavesdropping indicated that Max and Captain Peggy took the lead.

A few days after the sheriff's announcement Max said; "Well, I got the last of my traps moved back into our waters today. Let's see if those boys all do the same."

Captain Peggy added; "I saw one of their boats removing traps from our waters when I was returning with mine from the area they claim. I gave the guy a little wave and he returned it, but he didn't smile. They can't be happy, we pushed them hard."

It was now too cold many afternoons to sit outside on the deck so I generally stayed inside upstairs as I still felt out of place sitting with the lobstermen in the Pub. I had been wrong about Red being responsible for Rob's death but relieved that the island's lobstermen were no longer suspected of having a part in his death.

Amanda had told me the Portland office had no

knowledge of Red and had no idea where he might be living. The Portland detectives suspected Red lived elsewhere and stayed with Roxy and maybe some other women when he was in Portland.

News of Amanda's involvement must have traveled fast as she told me Danny had not been contacted by Red about another delivery. It appeared that Red had either found another boat or the offshore delivery system using Rob's boat had been terminated.

The trail had gone cold and it appeared Red had disappeared - or so it seemed.

22

4th Week of October

The trees were almost bare by the last week of October. The Inn was no longer very busy and most days I was the only guest. Anne couldn't offer a new person much work so from time-to-time Sally would still show up to do some cleaning.

On Monday afternoon Sally asked if we could talk.

"Mr. Wilson, Red called Roxy again yesterday and she decided to talk to him. It was a serious mistake and Red threatened both Roxy and me. He said we would regret it if we ever talked to that deputy or police woman again. Roxy told me the call was very scary!"

"Red seems to know about everything we do or say and we are really frightened. I shouldn't be talking to you but you need to tell that investigator why we can't talk to her again."

Sally didn't wait for an answer - she just walked out the door.

I called Amanda and told her about Sally's visit and Sally's request that Amanda not contact either Roxy or Sally in the future. Amanda said she would respect their request for the time being but she asked;

"How do you think Red found out about my visits with Roxy and Sally? I haven't even told you anything about those visits and I seriously doubt either of them told him."

Amanda added; "I wouldn't be surprised if Danny told Red about my visit with him. Danny is more afraid of Red than me. I certainly didn't tell Danny about talking with Roxy, Sally or you."

I responded; "Amanda, it could be that Red was just guessing and got a reaction from Roxy or Red has another source of information in Stone Harbor."

I asked; "Do you think Red might be hanging around Stone Harbor? He certainly is the most likely person to have slashed my tires."

Amanda replied; "That's very possible but he is certainly keeping a low profile."

#   #   #

Conversations around Stone Harbor that last week of October had shifted to the upcoming winter weather. A few folks that could afford winter vacations talked about future trips to warmer climates. Dave's confession was now old news and the rumors indicated that since he confessed and didn't intend to kill Rob he would be charged with manslaughter not murder.

The lobstermen had all retreated to undisputed waters and talk of a lobster war was no longer a topic of conversation.

Amanda and I were both relieved that no rumors were circulating about Red, Roxy or Sally. Amanda was working several other cases and I didn't see her as often around Stone Harbor that week. When I saw Sally at the Inn she told me Roxy had not had any more calls or conversations with Red.

Everything seemed to be quiet - maybe too quiet.

#   #   #

Despite the distractions, I was making steady but slow progress on writing my novel. My relationship with Anne was getting better by the day. I enjoyed being with Anne and decided to ask if she wanted to join me for an outing and drive to visit Acadia National Park. I had visited the park in July when it was packed with tourists and I wanted to visit the park's dramatic coastline again when there would be much less traffic.

Anne accepted my invitation and we drove to Bar

Harbor for lunch on Wednesday and then started the drive along the coast road in the park.

Anne was really excited and I discovered she had never actually visited the park. She exclaimed; "These views are magnificent!"

Acadia Shoreline

With essentially no other traffic on the one-way coast road we were able to stop frequently to enjoy the views. We also stopped at a number of parking areas to take short walks along the top of the rocky cliffs.

The late October wind was rather cold so we only took short walks along the cliffs overlooking the ocean. We enjoyed a bit longer walk with less wind along one of the trails in the woods. I was pleased that Anne frequently reached for my hand.

I was distracted by our conversation as we slowly drove along the left hand lane to get a better view of the shoreline and didn't pay much attention to a black SUV pulling along our right side to pass.

"Shit!" was all I had time to say as the SUV slammed into the passenger side of my rental car and forced us off the road toward the cliffs along the shoreline. But this time I had clearly seen the grin on Red's face as he forced us off the road.

The airbags deployed as my car crashed through a wooden guardrail and some underbrush along the walking trail beside the road. The terrain was very steep and the car rolled over but thankfully landed right side up as my driver's side came to rest against a large boulder.

I was stunned and unable to move but could see through the broken windshield that someone was now standing up on the road looking down at our car. That person was joined by a second person that started down the embankment toward our car.

"Anne, are you OK?"

"No, I don't know and it hurts to move."

Just then a stranger approached the car and asked if we were OK. I answered; "No, please get help."

"My wife is calling 911, stay calm. Help will arrive."

A short while later a Park Ranger and ambulance arrived. They needed to use some special equipment to open the doors, get us out of the car and onto stretchers. I really don't remember much about the next hour or so until my head cleared while lying on a table in the emergency room.

I asked one of the doctors about Anne and was told; "You keep asking that same question. She just has minor cuts, bruises and a broken right arm but otherwise seems OK. You are in about the same condition but you suffered a broken left arm and a possible concussion. We'll keep you both overnight and assess you both again in the morning."

I asked; "What happened and who came to our rescue?"

"You need to rest and talk to the Park Rangers tomorrow."

"OK, but please call Amanda Smith at the Stone Harbor sheriff's office and tell her what happened."

*   *   *

When I awoke Thursday morning I saw Amanda sitting next to my bed. As I opened my eyes she said; "Hi, feeling better?"

"Can I answer that later? Right now I just hurt everywhere. How is Anne? Is she OK?"

"Anne is in better shape than you - she suffered cuts, bruises and a broken right arm. I just talked to her and she is sitting up and eating some breakfast."

Amanda then asked; "What happened?"

"I wasn't paying enough attention and a black SUV pulled up beside us and forced us off the road. Amanda, this time I am certain the driver was Red."

Amanda replied; "When I arrived yesterday afternoon I was given the name and contact information for Mr. Williams, the man that helped you. He told me that he and his wife had rounded a curve and saw a man standing beside an SUV looking down toward the ocean."

"They stopped to see what was happening and the man said he just saw a car go off the road and was just getting ready to call 911. Mr. Williams said the man told him to head on down to help and he would join him after he talked to 911."

"So Williams headed down the slope to your car and when he turned around the man was gone. He said he shouted up to his wife to call 911 and then tried to help you but it was impossible to open the car doors."

"I also asked if I could talk to his wife. When she

got on the phone I asked her about the man. She said the moment her husband started down the slope the man got in his SUV and drove off."

"I then asked her for a description of the driver. She said everything happened very fast but she was certain the man had red hair."

"I asked if I could text or email a picture to them and they said a text was fine since they were still traveling on vacation and were using their cell phones. They both identified Red as the driver of that SUV."

"This time it looks like you were right. You and Anne were very lucky."

23

Late Thursday Amanda made certain that the hit-and-run bulletin contained a description and a photo of Red. However, no trace was found of either the black SUV or Red.

We still didn't even know his name and assumed Red was just a nickname because of his red hair. Amanda had been discussing the case with her counterparts in Portland but they also had uncovered no information concerning Red. So far everything had been a dead end.

Amanda was puzzled as to why Red would even risk running us off the road. Killing me would accomplish nothing. Why was this so important?

In any event, his picture was on the hit-and-run bulletin and his actions had made him a wanted man. It would be difficult for him to keep out of sight.

Anne and I were both released from the hospital in Bar Harbor later that day and Amanda drove us back to the Inn.

#   #   #

Friday morning Sally knocked on my room door.

"Mr. Wilson, are you OK? Will you talk to Roxy again?"

"Yes, certainly. When and where?"

"She's downstairs."

"Let's go down and talk with her."

"No, I will go down and bring her up to your room. Roxy doesn't want to take any chances that someone will see you together."

Sally and Roxy entered my room a few minutes later and Roxy looked at Sally and again said; "Get lost."

"Mr. Wilson, I am so sorry you got hurt by Red. I'm really scared and want him captured. I think I might know something that can help you find him."

"Roxy, you should talk to Amanda."

"No, I don't trust the police. I am certain Red has a spy and will find out if I talk to anyone in the police again."

"Why do you think Red has a spy?"

"I overheard him talking to someone one night on his cell phone and he said "Don't worry, I can let you know if the cops plan anything, I have sources"."

"What else can you tell me that might help?"

"Red knows that his red hair makes it easy to identify him. He frequently wears wigs with different colored hair, sometimes a fake mustache and old clothes to fool people."

"How do you know?"

"He was wearing a wig the night I met him in that bar and he always wore a wig when we went out to a bar or dinner. We also never went to the same place twice. He didn't want people to remember him."

"Didn't you think that was a little strange?"

"Mr. Wilson, I'm not a fool. It was obvious Red had something to do with drugs but he was mostly nice to me and it was exciting to this small town girl."

"Do you think he has been hanging around Stone Harbor?"

"Yes, that's why I'm afraid."

"Why do you think he ran me off the road?"

"Red hates you. He was talking on his cell phone the night before he lost his temper and hit me. I don't know who he was talking to but he said; "Don't worry I'll fix that Wilson guy. He won't screw up our business"."

"When he got off the phone he was really angry and said, "That bastard Wilson just doesn't learn - he won't mess with me again"."

"That's when he asked me to have Sally take some photos of the pages in your notebook."

"He completely lost it when I told him the next day that Sally wouldn't do it. That's when he started hitting me and said she damn well better do it!"

"He stormed out of my apartment and I was so scared I drove back home."

"Let me ask you again, do you know his name or where he might live?"

"No, I really don't know. He always came to my apartment and said his friends just called him Red."

"How did you contact him?"

"I didn't, he never had the same phone or number. He always called me."

"Did he ever use a credit card or be asked to show identification?"

"He always paid cash and I don't ever remember him showing anyone a drivers license or ID card."

"Will you let the police examine your apartment for fingerprints or a toothbrush for DNA."

"It's too late, my apartment is already rented to someone else."

"Roxy, does Red carry a gun?"

"Yes, I have seen it several times."

"Is there anything else you want to tell me?"

"No, I just wanted you to know about the spy and I really think he wants to kill you. He was really angry about you messing with his business."

"Why tell me?"

"I won't be safe again until Red is in jail or dead. I don't know who it's safe to talk to and you are my best bet."

#   #   #

I took an hour or so to absorb what Roxy had told me before I called Amanda.

"Amanda, I think we need to talk. Can you come over to the Inn."

"I am not in Stone Harbor at present but I can talk to you this evening if it's important."

"It's important."

Amanda arrived that evening and we sat in the empty living room; I was uncomfortable suggesting she come to my room.

"Amanda, Roxy came to my room today to talk about Red. She said she will never be safe until he's in jail or dead."

"Roxy told me that she believes Red has a spy in the police department. That would explain how Red seems to know who you talk to and what information you have shared."

"She also told me he has a very bad temper and is very angry that I won't stop messing in his business. She believes he is angry enough to want me dead. That would explain pushing my car off the road in Acadia."

"She also said he frequently wears a wig and other disguises to hide his red hair and make it difficult to identify him. She believes he is hanging around Stone Harbor and that's why she is so afraid."

Amanda sat in silence for a few minutes and then asked; "Do you believe her? Why did she come to you?"

"Roxy said she didn't trust talking to you because Red has an informant and he would find out."

Amanda was again silent for a few minutes and then replied;

"Roxy might be right. I have written rather detailed reports for our files and I share those reports with the investigators in Portland so they will know what I know about Red's possible activities. Interesting that he seems to know about my conversations with Roxy and Sally. That might also be why he stopped contacting Danny."

"Some of my information came from your conversations with Roxy and Sally but I did not site you as the source. I have not included any reference to our conversations in my reports and he doesn't seem to know that I talk to you."

"I won't write a report about this conversation."

Then Amanda surprised me; "I've had a long week and I am hungry. Let's go to dinner, I'm off duty."

"OK, I'll get my car keys. The rental car folks were nice enough to deliver a new car for me today."

"Not necessary, I'll drive and it's probably safer since you just got out of the hospital and have a broken arm. I'm only supposed to use my unmarked car for official business but they expect me to use it for some personal trips when I am out of town."

Amanda drove us to a nearby cafe/bar a few miles out of town. It wasn't fancy but she said she thought it had good food.

We got some "looks" from several men at the bar when we walked in and sat down together in a fairly private corner booth.

I asked; "Have you been here before? I noticed the guys at the bar gave us the once over when we walked in."

"Stopped here once but I don't recognize anyone and no reason they would know me or what I do. As you know, I am never in uniform when I work in the field."

My reply sounded stupid; "They probably wanted to know what an old guy like me is doing with such an attractive, younger woman."

Amanda didn't laugh but said; "Don't sell yourself short and I am older than most people think."

The waitress came over to take our order and we

both ordered a beer and a cheese burger with fries.

"Is it OK if I ask how you became an investigator?"

"Sure, after college in Maine I went to law school in Boston. It was probably the books I read or the movies I watched but I always wanted to be a detective. I thought a law degree would be a good backup plan."

"I grew up in Portland and applied to every police department in Maine for an investigator's job. The county sheriff offered me a nice position and I have been with the department for almost fifteen years."

I was quietly trying to guess her age when she added;

"You don't need to guess; I know I dress and look much younger but I will be forty my next birthday."

Amanda was right - it was hard to believe this woman that looked like she was still in college would soon be forty.

I asked; "To be fair, do you want to know my background?"

Amanda replied: "I already know you have had a remarkable audit career for a small town kid from Kentucky."

"I have noticed that you always refer to yourself as a retired accountant and never talk about what you did or about banking in general."

I replied; "The 2007-2009 recession and housing crisis hurt many families and banking is no longer a respected profession. An amazing number of strangers seem to think I should know the answers to all their questions about what went wrong with our financial system. As a result, I have just found it best to avoid all such conversations."

Our burgers arrived and we enjoyed small talk for the rest of the evening.

24

1st week of November

It was now the first week of November, the "Leaf Peepers" were gone, the weather was much colder and the Inn was empty except for me.

Amanda called me Monday morning and said she wanted to stop by the Inn to talk with Anne and me. When Amanda arrived she asked if we could talk in Anne's apartment at the back of the Inn.

Once we were all seated Amanda said; "We are all worried about your safety. This Red person seems intent on harming Steve."

"Steve, the county sheriff and I agree that you are Red's target and we don't think it's safe for you to remain in Stone Harbor. We suggest that it's in Anne's best interest if you go back to New York."

"Anne, we have no reason to believe Red has any interest in harming you. You just happened to be with Steve in Acadia and you were just, as we say, collateral damage."

"Anne, the sheriff and I think you are safe remaining in Stone Harbor so long as Steve returns to New York."

I felt like I was deserting both Anne and Amanda but Amanda was very skillful and had made Anne's safety the basis for my departure. I had no choice but to respond;

"OK, I really don't want to leave but I will go back to New York if you think it is best for Anne's safety. But, looking at both Amanda and Anne, please keep me posted."

Amanda said; "OK, go pack your things. Book a flight and I will pick you up in an hour and drive you to Bangor. The deputy will make arrangements to return your rental car."

On our drive to Bangor, Amanda told me she had never been to New York City and she asked me about restaurants, Broadway theater, art galleries, neighborhoods and my apartment.

Amanda stayed with me until my flight arrived and I cleared security. I don't know if she enjoyed my company or just wanted to make certain I boarded the flight.

#   #   #

I was really bored the first few days after returning to New York. I had called Mark about dinner but he was out of town until later in the week.

I called Anne each day but she had no news and our conversations were very friendly but short. Her cuts and bruises were healing quickly and we both expected to have the cast on our arms removed by Thanksgiving.

I called Nancy and was pleased that we had a very pleasant visit. She was happy to be back teaching and said she had great students. The college had been very understanding about her "family emergency" after she told them what had actually happened with her photos. She was clearly relieved that she had received no other threats relating to the missing photos.

I called Amanda but she provided no meaningful updates on Red. She did ask about New York and encouraged me to enjoy the city.

Amanda had a real talent for asking questions and not sharing any information.

I couldn't concentrate on my book. Shortly after I had arrived in Stone Harbor I had decided to write my novel based on a money-laundering case that utilized the international banking system and cryptocurrency. It seemed like a timely topic and it had been a fascinating case to solve. I had made some progress but current events had seriously diverted my attention.

I tried to shift my attention to my hobby of researching old maps without much success. During my travels in Maine I had stopped at a number of shops that sold old maps and nautical charts. Each of these documents tells a story in time and I have always enjoyed researching history. I admired these early explorers and their fearless nature.

I received a call from another unknown number on Thursday afternoon and, as usual, I did not answer. I just get too many calls to lower my credit card interest rate or win a free vacation.

When I heard the ping indicating a message I listened to the message.

"Steve, don't be stupid! If you know what's best for Anne you will return to Stone Harbor."

Mark had returned to New York that morning and we had already planned dinner that night. I decided to talk with Mark before I told Amanda about the new phone message.

We walked to a neighborhood restaurant and after we were seated I started the conversation.

"Mark, I received another message today. Please listen to it."

After listening he responded; "This guy sounds

really angry and is acting stupid. Do you think he would really harm Anne?"

"Yes. It looks like he blames my persistence for messing up his business. Still strange that it has made him mad enough to seek revenge. Do you think it's something more?"

Mark replied; "Might be something else - not just messing with his business. But, in any event, you need to call Amanda and return to Stone Harbor. Like it or not you are now the bait to flush out this guy Red."

#   #   #

I called Amanda early Friday morning and briefed her on the message and my dinner with Mark. She responded;

"Steve, I agree you should probably return to Stone Harbor but I don't like it. Don't rent a car and drive this time."

"Book a flight to Bangor for tomorrow and I will pick you up and drive you back to the Inn."

Amanda met my flight on Saturday morning and on the drive back to Stone Harbor she was more forthcoming about her thoughts.

"The county sheriff and I discussed Roxy's belief

that Red has a spy somewhere. We really looked at every possibility in our department and we concluded the spy must be located in Portland."

"The county sheriff and I had a face-to-face meeting with the senior officers in Portland earlier this week to discuss the matter. We decided that I would submit a false report that afternoon that said we had located Red and planned to arrest him that night."

"The Portland investigator would then watch the reaction of everyone who had access to my report in the normal flow of business that afternoon."

"Red's spy took the bait. When the file clerk looked at the report she panicked and made an excuse to go outside to her car. Our investigator followed her and overhead her leave a message for her husband saying that we had located Red and planned to arrest him. She told her husband he had better warn Red."

"The investigator confronted the clerk and escorted her back into the building to be interrogated. She was not placed under arrest and was asked if she was willing to cooperate. She said she would cooperate if they would agree not to arrest her husband for using drugs. They agreed to her request and she started talking."

"First, she was asked to call her husband and tell him she had been discovered and she had agreed to cooperate. If her husband had already contacted Red he should call him back and tell him, "Sorry, it was a false alarm". If he hadn't contacted Red he should not do so under any circumstance. We didn't want to alert Red to any activity until we learned more and had a plan."

"The clerk said her husband had been hurt at work several years ago. When the doctors stopped prescribing his pain medicine he found another source of opioids."

"The clerk admitted her husband was hooked on opioids and Red controlled the source. When Red learned she worked in the sheriff's office he said he would provide her husband free drugs when she provided helpful information."

"The clerk said that most of the time they paid cash for opioids that were delivered by a dealer who apparently worked for Red. But one night while her husband was at work, Red delivered the drugs personally to thank her for some information she had provided and that night he had also demanded sex in return for the drugs."

"When she was asked about the last time she had seen Red, she responded it had been the previous night when her husband was at work."

"When asked, the clerk gave permission for Portland investigators to examine their apartment for fingerprints."

"The investigators processed fingerprints from a glass and some DNA samples and made a positive identification."

"Red's name is Larry Spencer. He is reported to live in Boston and to work with one of the international drug cartels. His fingerprints were put on file after he was arrested for possession several years ago in a minor drug bust. Other than that arrest he does not have a record."

Amanda also told me she had obtained court permission to place a GPS tracking devise on Rob's boat but the boat had not moved and no offshore deliveries had occurred since Amanda had placed the device near the helm.

I asked Amanda to stay around for a while after we arrived at the Inn as I wanted to review some of my notes with her. We adjourned to the empty living room after I said hello to Anne and placed my travel bag in my room.

"Amanda, I still think there is more to this story and I want to review my thinking with you. As I learn new information I always try to update my timeline of events. Please take a look at this list of dates based on what we know and the information

Roxy has provided."

Wednesday:	Rob and Red on Rob's boat - with 4 totes
	Rob's boat returns to dock - with 2 totes?
Thursday:	Rob departs alone on his boat Dave kills Rob, fakes accident Max finds Rob's empty boat - 2 totes
Saturday:	Max discovers Rob's body
Monday:	Mary Alice visits the Pub When did Red learn about the visit?
Wednesday:	Nancy's photos displayed at library Mary Alice overdose - source/Red?
Thursday:	Neighbor discovers Mary Alice's body Red learns about photos from Sally
Friday:	Sally takes photos from Library Sally takes photo of Nancy's registration card
Saturday:	Nancy gets phone call from Red

"Amanda, I was so focused on what was in those bait totes and on Red's potential involvement in Rob's death that I overlooked his potential relationship to Mary Alice's overdose."

"I had suspected that Red was involved in dealing drugs but we had no confirmation until I spoke to Roxy."

"But, we still don't know when Red learned about Mary Alice's visit to the Pub. Did he learn about her visit before or after she had her overdose?"

"I think it's time I have another conversation with Roxy."

Amanda agreed and said:

"We don't want to tell Roxy about learning the identity of the informant until we apprehend Red. So I agree it's still best if you talk to Roxy alone. Just keep me posted."

25

2nd week of November

It was now the second week of November and my original plan to depart Stone Harbor in mid-September was long past. I certainly had never anticipated getting involved in a local criminal investigation.

I didn't want to contact Sally directly and asked Anne to call Sally and ask her to come to the Inn.

Sally came to the Inn Sunday morning and I asked;

"Sally, do you think Roxy will talk to me again?"

"Don't ask me, I will call her."

Roxy agreed and appeared alone at my door a short while later. She requested we meet privately again as she still didn't trust anyone but was relieved that Red didn't seem to know about our last visit and conversation about the spy.

"Roxy, I want to ask some more questions about Mary Alice."

"OK, sure."

I asked; "Roxy, you told me Red was the source of drugs for Mary Alice. Correct?"

Roxy replied; "Yes, but you need to understand. Red only delivered drugs in person when he traded sex for drugs. He was not a street dealer but Mary Alice told me Red had arranged for someone to deliver her opioids for cash."

I asked; "Do you know who that local dealer is?"

"No, and I didn't want to know so I never asked her."

"Why couldn't Mary Alice get more heroin after Rob's death?"

"She called me that day she went to the Pub. She told me she didn't know where Rob kept the cash. Said she looked everywhere and the local dealer would only deliver for cash. She needed to talk to Red."

"She told me she had tried to call Red but the number she had was disconnected. Red just used those pre-paid throw away phones and never used the same phone for any length of time."

"Did you give her his number?"

"I just had the same old number she did and, anyway, he told me to never call him. He always called me if he was in town and wanted to see me."

"Do you recall when Red learned about her visit to the Pub?"

"Sure, it was later the same night Mary Alice went to the Pub. When he came to my place I had just talked to Sally. She said the rumor was spreading fast."

I could tell this line of questioning was making Roxy nervous but I persisted.

"What did Red say or do that night?"

"He just said it was stupid of her to be talking like that at the Pub and he said he could make arrangements to help her."

"What do you think he meant?"

"Honestly I thought he was going to drive to Stone Harbor to trade sex for some heroin again. I'm certain they traded sometimes when she was in Portland to see me."

"Did you know Mary Alice died of an overdose of fentanyl?"

"Yes, I've heard that."

"Do you think Red gave that fentanyl to Mary Alice?"

"I didn't then but I do now - that's why I am so afraid."

26

Amanda returned to Stone Harbor on Monday and I briefed her on my conversation with Roxy.

Amanda responded; "Fentanyl is a lot more potent than heroin and is frequently mixed with heroin and linked to an overdose. If Red gave that fentanyl to Mary Alice then he should have just let well enough alone and not brought attention to himself."

"It looks like he might have panicked if he had just given Mary Alice an overdose of fentanyl and then found out that photos of him with Rob on Rob's boat were on display at the library."

"He was probably as bewildered as everyone else when Rob turned up dead. With Rob dead his delivery system for those bait totes was unexpectedly shut down and he would no longer be paying Rob to make deliveries. No deliveries by Rob meant no cash for Mary Alice to pay for her heroin."

"Red shouldn't have expected anyone to really care about those three photographs. All three were still shots and it just looked like two guys working on a lobster boat at a dock."

"It was stupid for him to threaten Nancy. He must have panicked and thought he could intimidate her and destroy any evidence that he had been personally acquainted with Rob."

"Steve, your curiosity about Nancy's missing photos and your persistence was his downfall. I now understand why he hates you."

Amanda then told me; "There has been no communication between Red and the file clerk or her husband since the spy relationship was uncovered. It is now past time for her husband's new drug delivery but they have not been contacted by the the street contact or by Red as expected."

"Red had always provided the husband with a number to call when he had important information but that number is now dead."

Amanda added; "The Portland sheriff had hoped to arrest Red if he showed up to to trade sex for drugs with the clerk. However, Red has been silent and is a no show in Portland."

Amanda concluded; "We think it's time we try to

flush Red out of hiding."

#   #   #

On Tuesday Amanda stopped by the Inn.

"Steve, this morning we issued a warrant for Red's arrest on suspicion of murdering Mary Alice. We published both his name and his photo and hope this will flush him out of hiding. I will keep you posted."

"I want both you and Anne to continue to stay inside the Inn for your safety. We don't want Red to have any opportunity to make one last attempt to get revenge."

On Friday I was debriefed by Amanda.

"The GPS on Rob's boat started moving Wednesday night and the GPS signal was tracked by a Coast Guard vessel from a distance of over fifteen miles so as not to be seen."

"The deputy and I drove out to Rob's dock to confirm the boat was actually gone. The boat was gone and a black pickup was parked next to the dock."

"We had a lab guy come out that night and take fingerprints. He confirmed that Red's fingerprints were all over that pickup."

"The GPS on Rob's boat had headed offshore and then stopped moving in international waters. The Coast Guard vessel then went dark, no lights, so they could close in and monitor the situation better on their long-range radar. They determined that Rob's boat had met another vessel and that the two vessels were apparently side-by-side for about thirty minutes."

"At that time the other vessel headed north toward Nova Scotia and Rob's boat remained stationary in the water."

"The Coast Guard notified the Nova Scotia Coast Guard that a suspicious vessel possibly associated with the drug trade was headed their direction."

"The Coast Guard vessel was then given permission to approach Rob's boat and, as an excuse, to offer assistance if necessary. When they arrived it was determined that Rob's boat had it's engine running but was not in gear and underway. The Coast Guard sent several people over to Rob's boat to inspect it and they determined that once again Rob's boat was deserted."

"The Coast Guard vessel towed Rob's boat back to Stone Harbor and it was tied up at the town dock Thursday afternoon."

"Also, this morning we received an interesting report from the Nova Scotia Coast Guard. They intercepted the other vessel, a fishing trawler, before it entered port. They questioned every crew member but they found no sign of Red."

"However, based on your suspicions, they also inspected every bait tote onboard. You were right, they discovered almost $10 million in cash hidden in three bait totes."

"However, they found no evidence of illegal drugs on that vessel."

"The crew is being held for questioning and, according to the Nova Scotia folks, two of the crew members don't appear to be working seamen."

#   #   #

I was relieved to know I was right about the contents of the bait totes but we were all mystified by the location of Red as he had yet to surface.

Was it possible that one of the men on the fishing trawler had met Red on shore and then that man made the delivery of the bait totes? They could have swapped vehicles and Red was still in Maine. Roxy was right, none of us would be safe until Red was apprehended.

That afternoon I walked to the town dock with Amanda. The deputy had once again placed the yellow "do not enter" tape around Rob's boat.

Amanda had been granted court permission to inspect the boat and I watched as she carefully examined every inch of the vessel. A lab technician took fingerprints from the steering wheel and navigation equipment to determine if they could identify who had taken the boat offshore.

There were no remaining bait totes on the deck but I pointed out a large bait barrel and I suggested Amanda open it. Her rather sarcastic reply was;

"Thanks, but that stuff really stinks so I plan do that last!"

Finally she was done with her inspection and moved to the bait barrel to open it. When she did so I heard her gasp and swear!

"What the fuck!"

Amanda had just discovered a body in the bait barrel!

The Medical Examiner's report on Saturday morning identified that body as Larry Spencer, the man we called Red. His hands had been tied behind his back, he had major bruises and had been shot in the back of the head execution style.

#   #   #

Amanda was busy with reports the next few days

at the county sheriff's office and debriefings with both the Coast Guard and the Portland sheriff's office. She also talked with my friend Mark at the FBI but neither of them would reveal the nature of their conversation - just official business. I must admit, I don't like being an outsider.

I was pleased when Amanda took time to call me when her work was concluded and asked me to join her for dinner.

On our drive to dinner Amanda said; "We got word from Boston that the cartel folks didn't like Red acting on his own and killing Mary Alice without permission. His actions were bringing too much attention to their activities and they wanted to set an example. That's why he was executed."

After that update we arrived at another out-of-town restaurant for a very enjoyable dinner together. Amanda was very grateful for the help I had provided her and indicated everyone was very pleased with her work on the case.

"Steve, I have really enjoyed getting to know you and working with you on this case. I hope you keep in touch and we can remain friends. It would be nice if we could actually work together again."

"I agree, Amanda. I will stay in touch and maybe we can arrange that visit to New York sometime."

27

Thanksgiving Week

I was pleased that Anne asked me if I wanted to stay at the Inn for the Thanksgiving holiday.

I had responded; "Yes, thank you, that will give me an opportunity to work on my book for a few quiet days."

Anne had decorated the Inn and hosted an open house on Thanksgiving morning for her friends in the community. Dozens of people showed up at the Inn for holiday treats and a little wine.

I didn't realize it at first but Anne's arrangements on Thanksgiving Day were intended to be a "Thank You" to me from some of the folks in Stone Harbor. I was pleased that Roxy, Sally, Sandy and Kathy were among the group that showed up that morning to say thanks for helping solve the mystery surrounding the deaths of their friends Rob and Mary Alice.

Roxy made a special point of talking to me. "Mr.

Wilson, both Mary Alice and Rob were my friends. I really screwed up, if I hadn't introduced Mary Alice to Red she wouldn't have gotten hooked on heroin and they would both still be alive."

I replied; "Don't be too hard on yourself. Mary Alice was already dependent on a prescription drug. It's become all too easy to find a street source for opioids to replace the prescriptions. It's not your fault that our entire country has such a serious opioid problem."

That afternoon Anne prepared a couple of turkeys with all the traditional extras. The Inn had a larger kitchen than I expected and Anne was a wonderful cook. I tried to help her but I was most likely a nuisance.

The afternoon group included Captain Max and his wife, Captain Peggy and her husband, Barbara and her husband, the deputy sheriff and his wife, Anne and me. Anne's breakfast room was now set up with a large table for all of us to enjoy Anne's delightful Thanksgiving dinner together.

#   #   #

The next day the Inn was empty and Anne seldom opened for guests during the winter. It was time for me to return to New York.

So on Friday morning I rather awkwardly approached Anne.

"Anne we have had a real mix of highs and lows over the past four months and your broken arm has certainly been a poor reminder of our friendship."

"It's time for me to return to New York but I want you to know I will miss your company."

Once again we had an awkward silence between us.

Then Anne replied; "I will miss being with you as well. I certainly botched that first dinner alone together and hope Thanksgiving helped make amends."

I asked: "Anne, would you be interested in visiting me in New York sometime?"

Anne replied; "How about next week?"

EPILOGUE

I was pleased that Anne accepted my invitation to join me in New York. We dined in nice restaurants, attended Broadway shows, visited art and history museums and enjoyed the festive holiday season. Anne had also made plans to enjoy some warm weather with her friends in Florida after our Christmas together in New York.

Anne had surprised me the day after she arrived in New York with a suggestion:

"Steve, we have talked several times about how challenging it has been to write your first novel. Don't the events of the past several months provide you with an excellent plot for a good murder mystery? Why not base your story on the events in Stone Harbor?"

I thought Anne's suggestion was an excellent idea. So, as they say, I decided to change the names to protect the innocent and have based my first novel on my adventure in Stone Harbor.

I wanted Anne to meet Mark during her visit so I

invited Mark and his wife, Carol, to join us for a relaxing dinner. We all enjoyed a wide ranging discussion about restaurants, art museums, art history, Broadway theater and debated ideas for the title of my first book.

Mark concluded our discussions that evening with an intriguing question for me;

"Steve, have you ever considered going into business for yourself to help smaller community banks with fraud and money laundering investigations? They could use your help."

I replied; "No, I never thought about it."

Mark said; "You should. Amanda and I are working on a case with a bank in Maine that would benefit from your experience."

"Mark, that might be interesting but right now I want to finish my book and enjoy the holidays. If it works for you we can talk in early January."

Mark replied; "That works for me."

DEATH TRAP

Acknowledgements

Our visits to Maine over the past decade have provided me with extensive information about DownEast Maine and insight into the independent nature, courage and dedication of Maine's lobstermen.

Death Trap required significant additional research to provide accurate descriptions of DownEast Maine and Maine's lobstermen. I am grateful for the additional background information I was able to obtain about lobster fishing, fishing equipment and lobster boat racing from the following:

Bangor Daily News
F/V Summerwind
Hamilton Marine, Marine Supplier
Maine Department of Marine Resources
Maine Lobster Boat Racing Association
Power & Motoryacht Magazine

Photos

Molly Potter Thayer

About the Author

Charles Thayer is the author of numerous business books and articles. Death Trap is his first work of fiction.

Charles and his wife, Molly, and their dog, Scupper, enjoy cruising along the east coast and visiting Maine aboard their Duffy 37, a Maine built lobster boat with a custom interior.

Charles enjoyed a fifty-year career in the banking industry having served as an executive officer and as a board member of several banking institutions.

Additional profile information is available on his Amazon author's page.

Previous Books

Charles J Thayer

2017   *Bank Director Survival Guide*
       Chartwell Publications

2016   *Credit Check*
       Giving Credit Where Credit Is Due

2010   *It Is What It Is*
       Saving American West Bank

1986   *The Bank Director's Handbook;*
       Auburn House: 2nd Edition
       Chapter: Asset/Liability Management

1983   *Bankers Desk Reference*
       Warren, Gorham & Lamont
       Chapter: Financial Futures Market

1981   *The Bank Director's Handbook;*
       Auburn House: 1st Edition
       Chapter: Asset/Liability Management

37721913R00136

Made in the USA
Columbia, SC
02 December 2018